It's Your Misfortune and None of My Own

G·K
Hall
&C?

*Also by Stephen Bly
in Large Print:*

The Stuart Brannon Western Series

Hard Winter at Broken Arrow Crossing
False Claims at the Little Stephen Mine
Last Hanging at Paradise Meadow
Standoff at Sunrise Creek
Final Justice at Adobe Wells
Son of an Arizona Legend

The Austin-Stoner Files

The Lost Manuscript of
  Martin Taylor Harrison

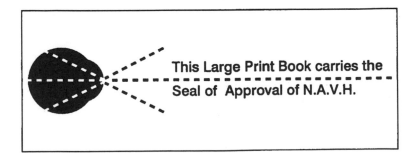

This Large Print Book carries the
Seal of Approval of N.A.V.H.

CODE OF THE WEST

BOOK ONE

IT'S YOUR MISFORTUNE AND NONE OF MY OWN

Stephen Bly

G.K. Hall & Co.
Thorndike, Maine

Copyright © 1994 by Stephen Bly

Published in 1997 by arrangement with Crossway Books, a
division of Good News Publishers.

G.K. Hall Large Print Western Collection.

The text of this Large Print edition is unabridged.
Other aspects of the book may vary from the original edition.

Set in 16 pt. Bookman Old Style.

Printed in the United States on permanent paper.

Library of Congress Cataloging in Publication Data

Bly, Stephen A., 1944–
  It's your misfortune and none of my own / Stephen Bly.
      p.   cm. — (Code of the West ; bk.#1)
  ISBN 0-7838-1787-8 (lg. print : hc)
  1. Large type books. I. Title. II. Series: Bly, Stephen A.,
1944–   Code of the West ; bk. 1.
  [PS3552.L93I87   1997]
  813'.54—dc20   96-11957

*For
JIM and JAN,
straight-shootin'
frontier friends*

1

September 1882, near the Kaibito River, Arizona Territory.

Brown eyes spied out from a dusty furrowed face appearing between a solid slab of granite and a gray beaver felt hat.

Through his worn duckings Tap Andrews felt sharp fragments of rock dig into his knees. Without ever taking his eyes off the horizon, he slipped five more .44-40 centerfire cartridges from his bullet belt and slid them systematically into the breech of his Winchester '73. Then he leaned it carefully beside him.

The column of dust in the distance rolled toward the rocky outcrop that was the only break in the high desert floor.

"They're goin' to charge us, ain't they?" a shaky voice called from somewhere to the lower left.

"Yep," Andrews acknowledged, "I reckon they will." The dry northern Arizona air tasted bitter, like the yellow and red desert that surrounded him.

"Are they Apaches?"

"Nope."

"How can you tell?"

" 'Cause were in Navajo country."

"We could sure use a couple dozen of them blue-coated cavalry boys!"

Tap dismissed the fear in the man's voice and mumbled, "I could sure use a cup of coffee."

Glancing back, he spotted the man in the dark vested suit crawling towards him.

"Don't you think we should concentrate on this side rather than keeping all spread out?" he asked.

"Stay where I put you. Shoot straight. Don't waste bullets," Andrews barked.

"This is crazy!" one of the hidden men cried out. "Five of us in these shallow rocks against two dozen mounted savages? We'll never survive! We ought to run for them mountains!"

"Black Mesa is fifty miles away," Andrews reported. His long legs began to cramp behind the scant boulder. He stretched them out along the ground and then repositioned himself on his knees.

"If that driver hadn't run those horses to death, we'd still be down there on the Utah road," a voice roared from under a torn black hat.

"I suppose yer blamin' me for the crossing being washed out too and us having to ride into this here swarm of mad Navajos?" the driver shouted back. "Look at them . . .

They're burnin' my stage! That's a $1,500 Concord!"

"And I say we try to talk to them!" another man called out. His voice sounded high-pitched, and his words ran together. "They must have mistaken us for someone else. I'm sure a few words could clear up this whole matter. Mr. Andrews, you do speak Navajo, don't you?"

Tap laid the round barrel of the '73 across the granite rock in front of him and took aim at the dust column still one thousand yards away. He flipped up the peep sight on the rifle and cranked it up to the top mark that had been filed on the gauge years before.

"Yeah, I can talk a little Navajo, but they aren't in a talkin' mood. They want a fight, and we happen to be in the wrong place at the wrong time."

"I still say we could —"

"Mister, if you don't have anything to do, you might want to scratch out a will, 'cause I'm tellin' you, these Indians are goin' to fight. Six days ago some men rode up to a hogan, smoked six Indians out, and shot 'em all, including four children. These fellas aim to settle that score."

"But we didn't do it! That's a matter for the sheriff or the army."

Andrews took a bead on the lead rider. "They don't intend to wait around and see if anything gets done, and I don't rightly blame 'em."

"You sidin' with those murderin' red-skins?"

"So far, only Indians have been murdered," Andrews grumbled. "But I assure you, I'll be tryin' to shoot them before they shoot me."

"Say . . . you ain't one of them? I mean, you're kind of dark-skinned yourself. Why . . . why, you could be an . . . an —"

"If you're plannin' on insultin' me, you'll have to call me something worse than an Indian," Andrews informed him.

"But we don't even know who you are and where you came from. What gives you the right to tell us what . . ."

One glance from Andrews and the man's voice trailed off in silence.

There was a puff of smoke in the distance and the sound of lead ricocheting off the boulders down below Andrews. Then the report of rifle fire echoed up off the desert floor.

"What are they tryin' to do from way back there?"

"Get us to reveal position," Andrews instructed. "Now, listen. I'm going to reduce the odds by one or two, but don't any of you fire until they ride up out of that draw. Let 'em keep guessing how many are up here."

"You can't hit anything from this distance!" another man shouted.

About that time several more wild shots slammed off the boulders behind them. The buzzing, ricocheting sound of bouncing lead gave way to silence.

Andrews pulled the hammer of the '73 back until the second click and then carefully set the sights on the brown shirt of the lead rider.

There was not even a wisp of a breeze. To Andrews it was as if nature was holding its breath until the battle began. He set the peep-hole sight on the man's chest and squeezed the trigger. At the same moment that the sound blasted in his ears he saw the distant rider tumble off his saddle and sprawl on the sand. The vibration of the explosion sent a sharp pain through his ear and down his right arm.

One of the men behind him whistled and shouted, "Good heavens, Andrews, you did it! You dropped him!"

Tap Andrews kept his sight on the next man who broke for the draw, and as the whole band charged forward, he draped another warrior on the desert floor. Cocking and repositioning the rifle, he reached up and rubbed his still aching ear.

No longer able to hold back for a good shot, the others fired wildly at the charging Indians. Smoke rose from the guns as from a campfire on a cold morning.

Lead pierced the desert stillness like needles attacking a pincushion.

Horses and men cried out.

The long-range sight was thrown back as Andrews fired at charging Indians. He could hear the man to the lower left scream out from his wounds, but there was no way to assist.

A shot from behind him forced him to dive for new cover.

They've busted through the backside! They must have shot the stage driver!

One warrior rode his paint horse right over the crest of the rocky knoll. Andrews rolled to the left and grabbed for his Colt. The startled Navajo swung to the right to take aim, but Tap fired two .44s, and the warrior dropped to the rocks.

Instantly, Andrews scrambled to his feet and grabbed the reins of the horse, swinging up into an old McClellan saddle. He charged right at the milling band of Indians. He took two more off their horses before they turned and retreated to the far side of the draw.

Reining up, he returned to the cover of the boulders, securing the Indian mount behind the largest of them. He could hear no fire from those who had stood with him, and to his surprise the Indians also ceased shooting.

One of the Navajo warriors held his rifle high above his head and rode boldly to the base of the rocks.

Not knowing if any were alive to hear him, Andrews yelled, "Hold up, boys! He wants to palaver!" He could feel the bitter smoke of gunpowder in the air sting his eyes.

"In the rocks!" the Indian yelled. "Come out, and let us discuss this!"

"We can hear you fine from here!" Andrews shouted back.

"We are leaving now!" the Navajo called out.

"That's mighty nice of you!" Andrews hollered as he shoved more shells into his Colt. He noticed the spokesman wore striped cavalry trousers.

"Is Yellow Rock dead?"

Andrews looked over at the injured Indian and noticed that he was laboring for breath. "He's still alive . . . barely!"

"We would like you to put him on his pony and send him down so that we may take him home."

"Kill him, Andrews!" he heard a weak voice call out from among the rocks.

Someone is alive!

"You want this old boy, you come up unarmed and get him. But you don't get the horse. I counted coup on Yellow Rock. The horse now belongs to me!" Andrews wiped the sweat off the back of his dirty

13

neck and felt his hair rub against his collarless cotton shirt.

The warrior turned and rode back.

"What's happenin', Andrews? I can't see 'em . . . What's goin' on?"

"They're talkin' it over."

"You goin' to let them hike up here and retrieve that Injun?"

"Yep."

"They're murderers!"

Andrews kept his eye on the band of warriors on the far side of the draw, half expecting them all to charge again. "There's dead on both sides, but nobody got murdered today. We were all armed. Besides, when you're outnumbered, you always let the other guy quit a fight!"

Soon the same Indian, stripped to the waist, walked up out of the draw to the base of the rocks. "I'm coming up to get Yellow Rock!"

"Keep your hands out in front of you!" Andrews instructed. Then turning to the rocky defense, he hollered loud enough for the Indian to hear, "Don't shoot him, boys. If he dies, we're all dead! Let him through."

All the way up the mountain, Andrews kept the Navajo covered with his rifle. Within moments the moccasin-booted Navajo stood in front of him. He glanced down at Yellow Rock lying on his stomach, unable to move his arms.

"You are a brave man," the Indian said in English.

"And so are you," Andrews spoke in Navajo.

"It was Yellow Rock's family who died at the hogan. It was his battle. We have our revenge. Now we will go home."

"You lost several warriors, too," Andrews noted.

"Yes . . . too many. You shoot very well with the Vernier tang sight." He motioned towards Andrews's '73. "Don't be surprised. I have ordered one for my own gun."

He hefted the severely wounded man to his shoulder. "You will not make it to Utah. We will see the pinto and ride out to stop you. There is no place to hide in the desert."

Andrews pointed the rifle at the man's head. "We'll make it."

"Your companions are all dead or dying, and you know it. It will be just you. We could charge up this mountain and kill you now."

"Go ahead and try it," Andrews taunted. "You'll be the first one to take lead."

"That's the problem. It would cost us two or three good men to kill you. We would rather kill you when there is no chance of us catching your bullets."

"Well, now that's mighty nice of you. I sure do thank ya for thinkin' of me."

"You are welcome." The Indian nodded

and hiked down the mountain, never looking back until he had joined the others on the far side of the draw. Within moments they had gathered up their dead and wounded and began riding across the desert to the distant hills.

Waiting until they were well out of gunshot range, Andrews stuck his hat on the end of his Winchester barrel and raised it slowly into full sight.

If they left one behind to take a potshot, this ought to give him a target.

Finally, Andrews jammed his hat on his head and stood up from behind the boulders. Carrying the Winchester across his arm, he surveyed the rock pile and found the stage driver and two others dead. Only the man with the deerskin coat was still breathing, although he had a severe wound in the shoulder and another in the leg.

Andrews helped the man down to the little clearing next to the paint horse.

"The others? Dead?"

"Yep."

"I don't think . . . I'm goin' to make it either," the man groaned.

"Well, it doesn't look good," Andrews said gently, "but the good Lord just might have a surprise for you."

"I'm ready . . . for that . . . Prop me up, would ya?"

Andrews scooted the man around so he could lean against a boulder. For a moment the man just stared at the rocks and gasped for breath. Finding a labored rhythm, he spoke. "Me and Jesus . . . settled up . . . a long time ago."

"You got a wife and kids?" Andrews asked. "Say, I don't think I got your name."

"Zach," he choked. "Zachariah Hatcher from Colorado. . . . You got any water?"

"Sorry," Tap apologized.

"I'm not married . . . I was on my way to meet my fiancée in Fort Collins. I . . . really need a drink."

By instinct Tap glanced around for a canteen, but both knew there was none.

"Can't believe I don't get to see her."

"Well, Zach, don't give up yet. We have a pony and some breathin' space. Maybe we can get you doctored and —"

"Mr. Andrews, I —"

"Tap. Just call me Tap."

"Tap? Like a hammer?"

"Tap . . . like in tapadera." He glanced around at the desolate rock pile. The smoke and dust caked his throat and made it difficult for him to swallow. "Now tell me about this special lady of yours."

"Never met her," Hatcher replied softly.

"What?"

"She's from Kentucky . . . We've been writin' for over two years."

"Writin'? You mean she's a *Heart-and-Home* woman?"

"No, not the magazine. I knew her brother, and I commenced to write . . . some time back."

"And you've never seen her?"

"Nope . . . too good to be true . . . everything working out so smooth. Bound to blow up on me. Tap, did you ever get a truly good break?"

"Eh . . . well, not many — no."

"Bought me a place up on the Wyoming line . . . came down to buy a couple good bulls from the Triple B Ranch —"

"You know Stuart Brannon?"

"He was gone . . . made a deal with one of his men. They'll ship them up in the spring. Fixin' to go settle down. And now this."

Andrews sat down beside the man and kept his eyes fixed on the declining sun across the Arizona horizon.

"That's a tough one, Hatcher. I can promise you I'll try to get you out of here."

The man closed his eyes, his lungs labored with every breath. "Headin' out of state, Mr. Andrews?"

"Eh . . . yeah, that's my intention."

"Runnin' from the law?"

"What?"

"I've seen men on the run. Catchin' the stage out in the open. Always lookin' back.

18

Never sayin' a word until those Indians attacked."

"Well, I was arrested for a murder I didn't commit. Either I run, or I rot down in Yuma."

"You got a place to go?"

"Anywhere away from Arizona, that's all."

"How about a side trip to Fort Collins? To find Suzanne."

"Suzanne?"

"Suzanne Cedar. My fiancée. She deserves to know that I didn't walk out on her. She's too nice a girl for that."

Andrews wiped the sweat from his full, dark eyebrows and allowed his hand to slide down across his face. "Yeah . . . I'll do that much for you." He glanced down at the wounded man. "Hatcher?"

The man opened his eyes. "Yes?"

"I thought . . . maybe you were gone. I'll go and tell the girl what happened. When were you supposed to meet her, and where?"

"It's in the letters."

"What letters?"

"In my saddlebags . . . a stack of letters, some money. Take 'em to her. She can sell the ranch and have enough to go back home . . . start a new life."

"Just in case those saddlebags didn't survive the stage fire, where were you going to meet her?"

"Wemberly House. Fort Collins . . . or on the road out to the Triple Creek Ranch if I'm late. That's my place . . . way out west of Virginia Dale you can . . ."

"Hatcher?" Andrews leaned over and listened to the man's rattling chest. "You got other kin up there I should notify?"

"Nope. I just bought the place . . . Don't know folk up there."

"How about back East? You want me to write to your mama and daddy?"

"They're gone . . . all gone. I expect to be seein' 'em soon enough. It's sure gettin' cold fast."

"Well, you got the faith — that's for sure. I'll tell that Cedar woman that you died believin'."

"Tell her to go back home . . . Tell her that, ya hear?"

"I hear ya."

"Land's too rough . . . a refined lady . . . all alone. I shouldn't have asked her to come . . . should never have got her hopes up. Andrews, are you there?"

Tap leaned over and put his hand on the man's forehead. "I'm here, Hatcher. I'm not leavin' ya."

"Are you there? Andrews! I can't feel nothin'! I can't see nothin'! Tell her I loved her, Andrews. Tell her I loved her more than anything in this whole world. The Lord will take care of her . . . He'll take care of her,

20

won't He, Andrews? Won't He?"

"Yeah, I reckon that's His job. He'll take care of her. Now you just —"

Andrews stopped. A broad smile broke across the man's face, temporarily dissolving the agony.

"Hatcher? What is it? Hatcher?"

He searched the man's neck for a pulse. Nothing.

Well, he either died thinking of that Miss Cedar . . . or Jesus . . . I guess there are worse ways to go.

For the next two hours Andrews carried all four bodies to the crest of the rocky knoll and stacked them together. Then he began to pile rocks over them.

"Boys, I suppose you all have gotten your rewards for this life by now, and since I didn't meet a one of you until this morning, I don't have much to say. This isn't the funeral. When I get to a town, I'll send 'em back to carry you off and bury you proper. But maybe this'll keep the buzzards and coyotes off. It ain't much, but it's the best I got. I hope there's someone around to do the same for me someday. We backed 'em down, boys. Someday they'll call these boulders Shootout Rocks or somethin'. Yes, sir, we backed the whole bunch down!"

Andrews smeared a few tears across his dirty face and jammed his gray hat back on his head. He sat down on the rocks, pulled off his boots, and dumped out pebbles and sand.

It's a mystery. A man wears fifteen-inch stove-top boots under his duckin's and still gets sand in there. I won't miss you, desert . . . I won't miss Arizona at all. . . . Oh, well, I might miss one or two of the ladies . . .

Yanking on his boots, he stood to his feet and walked over to the Indian pony. "Well . . . you are something. I grab myself a horse to ride out of here, and you're so shiny they could spot you in a dust storm on a moonless night! Now how am I goin' to prowl past those Navajos on a nickel-plated cayuse like you?"

Staying next to the rocks, Andrews slipped down the hillside and crawled over to the still-smoldering stagecoach. Most of the front of the coach was destroyed, but the back boot was partially intact. Several valises had escaped damage. He sorted through them and found a dark wool overcoat, a green blanket, a half-filled canteen, and saddlebags stamped "ZH."

"Well . . . I don't think anyone would complain if I allocated these for my own purposes. Hatcher, I'll carry these back to your girl, too."

He kept low and scurried back to the safety of the rocks.

They'll be out there. They'll be watching.

After dark he poured a little of his warm, stale water into his hat and let the horse lick it up. Then he pulled the old army saddle off the horse and tossed the green blanket over the pinto, stretching it from the horse's dark neck to the middle of its back. He let the long sides hang down, covering the horse to its knees. Then he sat the saddle and cinched it tight. Finally, he tied the long dark coat to the back of the saddle and let it hang over the rump of the pony.

"Well, old boy, not all your color is covered, but maybe we can slip past them in the night."

Sitting in the saddle, he tossed the saddlebags over his lap and laid the Winchester on top of them.

"Let's see what you got, Mr. Indian Pony. They know were headin' north. But I can't go south. By now every sheriff in the territory has got the news from Yuma!"

Riding the cuts, arroyos, and draws, Andrews meandered through the starlit desert.

There were no streams to cross.

No roads to follow.

No coyotes.

No trees.

No buildings.

And, Andrews was grateful to note, no Navajos.

By early daylight he walked the horse across a lightly traveled road that stretched north. He pulled the blanket and coat off and rubbed the sweat off the Indian pony. "You going to make it, boy? This old desert is hot enough without a heavy coat, isn't it?"

As he rode along, he dug through Zachariah Hatcher's saddlebags.

"Zach, you got any description of your place? I mean, Triple Creek Ranch isn't much to go by. Now I don't suppose you'd mind me using a little of this money to buy a new horse? Nothin' personal, old boy, but I can't ride one that can be seen for six miles! Well, I'll be . . . Here are those letters from his girl. He about wore them out."

Two men rode down the road toward him. He pulled back the hammer on his Winchester but left it lying on his lap. Then he tugged his hat low and avoided looking up with more than a tip of the hat as they passed.

A slight breeze from the northwest kept the desert sun at a tolerable level, and finally Andrews shoved his hat back and scanned the letters.

Her brother is . . . Abel . . . who seems to be out here somewhere. Maybe she can live with him? Feed store and horses in Kentucky . . . oh, here . . . She's twenty-two, but that was April 24, 1880. That makes her twenty-four. Rather tall? That's nice. I like tall women . . . golden hair. A pretty blonde? No, if she were a pretty blonde, she'd be married by now. 'Course, she might be a widow. Hatcher never said.

Baptist? Sings in the Baptist choir? Reads French novels! I bet she wears long, dark dresses and looks down her nose at "ruffians," no doubt. 'Course, Zachariah seemed to be a religious fellow. Maybe they would have made a pair.

Here's another . . . Virginia City, Montana? Zach drove cattle to Montana . . . She made a $12 quilt . . . sermons by Mr. Moody? Never heard of him. Friends getting married . . . scar? Hatcher has a scar? I didn't see any scar. She likes huntin' birds with a pump shotgun . . . got bucked off a bay mare. She sent him ginger cookies.

And this one says October . . . Father's sick . . . can't find Abel . . . photograph? She sent him a picture?

Andrews dug through the saddlebag. "Zach, there's no photograph in here, not of a lady . . . of the whole church choir?"

Probably has it in his vest. Wonder what she looks like. Sings, plays the piano, likes large families. Moving kind of quickly, but at her age I suppose you need to. . . . Afraid of violent men. He's supposed to send her a photograph.

Now in this one, father's dying . . . re-

ceived a photograph . . . "a little hard to see face under the hat," she says. Zach bought the ranch . . . She can talk to him better than other suitors. Zach, she's getting her spurs hooked in your flank. She asks about Mexican ladies. "Are they irresistibly beautiful?" You bet they are, darlin'. 'Course, I don't know what old Zachariah told you.

Picking out another letter, he carefully unfolded it. Her father died. Mother's moving to Chicago . . . selling the business. This is not a good year for Miss Suzanne Cedar. And the ranch sounds very "remote." Wants to bring out some horses, buy a piano . . . Here it is! She accepts the ring and agrees to marry him. I warned you, Zach. She caught you fair and square. She's a "tried-and-true romantic." Oh boy, you just might have lucked out by dying, Mr. Hatcher. This is no place for a romantic!

Now this one says he's in Prescott. She's spending the summer at her mother's in Chicago . . . coming to Denver . . . bringing her inheritance? An inheritance! Hatcher, you sly fox, you might have been right. Plain women can make good wives.

Here's the last one . . . okay, she'll be in Denver on the twentieth. That's next week. By Thursday she'll be in Fort Collins. Now she admits the choir picture wasn't all that good. Sure, now you tell him.

"I count every day and pray for each to

*speed along until we meet. I'm a little
scared to launch out into the frontier. You
will have to be my strength."*

Andrews folded the letters and shoved
them back into the saddlebags. "Well, darlin', you're goin' to have to find that
strength on your own. Hatcher was right
about one thing — this is no place for a
lady of your sensitivities."

A little past noon he rode into Mexican
Wells. The Arizona village was the last before the Utah border. Its remoteness provided a haven for those wanting to hide
from civilization.

He told the story of the shootout to the
owner of the cantina, who promised to send
some men out to bring back the bodies.
Then he traded in the pinto, McClellan, and
a few cash dollars for a tall brown horse
and a good Texas saddle.

"Some Indian might ride in here mad as
a rattler and claim that's his horse," he
advised the man.

"That's nothin'," the man roared. "If a
certain feller finds you on that brown, using
his saddle, you're goin' to wish you were
back with those Injuns!"

"Can I ride north with it?"

"Yep . . . but don't plan on bringing it
back to Arizona."

Andrews sat with his back to the wall on

27

a crate next to a table that had been broken and rebuilt more than once. Tossing the saddlebags across the table, he ordered something to eat. In a few minutes he was dipping a chunk of bread in some stew when a woman in a slightly soiled white dress walked right up to him and sat down.

"Well, if it isn't that Mr. Hatcher! You come back to see me?"

"Hatcher? You think I'm . . ."

Her eyes grew wide. "Hey, it's okay with me," she whispered in a coarse, abrupt way. "I mean, if you want another name, who am I to complain? My name ain't really Sassy, but you probably knowed that. You didn't change your mind, did ya? Or are you still all tied up with that Kentucky girl?"

Andrews swallowed a big piece of tough meat without chewing it. "Actually, darlin', I'm not . . ."

His voice trailed off when he looked up to see four dusty rifle-carrying men walk into the cantina. All four sported Deputy U.S. Marshal badges.

"You're not what?" Sassy pressed.

Andrews pulled his hat down and let his right hand drop to the walnut grip of his holstered .44. "Eh . . . I'm not all that hung up on . . . eh, Miss Cedar."

"Miss Suzanne Cedar! That's all you talked about last week. 'Course, I was feelin' my whiskey at the time . . . and you

28

was clean-shaven then," she admitted. "This Arizona sun must have done you good. You look even more handsome than before."

All four men walked carefully toward his table. He glanced at the exits, but he never looked at their faces.

"Say, mister," a deep voice boomed out.

Andrews reached over and clasped Sassy's arm with his left hand, at the same time slowly pulling back the hammer on his Colt with his right thumb.

"Why, Zachariah, I think they're talkin' to you." Sassy smiled.

Andrews glanced up at the lawmen. Without moving either hand, he broke into a wide grin. "You boys sure are interrupting some important business here between me and this . . . this beautiful lady — if you catch my drift!"

"We're lookin' for a man headin' north. You headin' north?"

"Yes, he is, but so what?" Sassy answered. "Who are you lookin' for?"

"An escaped murderer called Tapadera Andrews. Broke out of A.T.P. a few weeks ago, and we figure he's runnin' this way."

"It don't seem likely to me that anyone would escape from Yuma and not go down into Mexico." She scooted her broken chair over next to Andrews's and slipped her arm around his waist. "What's this fella supposed to look like?"

"Just about like this old boy eatin' the stew, that's what."

Sassy straightened the bust line of her dress and leaned her left elbow on the table, resting her chin in her hand. "What has he done to stir up so many brave and deadly deputy marshals?"

"He shot and killed a banker down in Globe City who happened to find him in a hotel with his wife."

"Whose wife?"

"The banker's wife!"

"Well, that certainly wasn't very sporting of either of them, was it? But this ain't Andrews. This here's Zachariah Hatcher. He's got this big ol' ranch up in Colorado . . . or Wyoming. Ain't that right, Zach?"

"Look, lady — and I use the term generously — I don't really give a hoot what you think —"

"You callin' this sweet darlin' a liar, are you?" Andrews pressed.

The man shrugged and turned toward Sassy. "You know this man?"

"Yep. He came down to buy some bulls from Stuart Brannon. He told me last time he was through. And I never forget a man who turns me down cold."

"Turned you down?"

"He wouldn't even buy me a drink and dance with me."

"That sure don't sound like Andrews. I

hear he always had an eye for the ladies," one of the deputies reported.

"See," she said, "look at his saddlebags. Z.H. That stands for Zachariah Hatcher."

"You know Brannon?" another deputy asked.

"Well . . . actually," Andrews stammered, "I, eh . . . bought the bulls, but Brannon was gone from the ranch at the time."

"So you did business with Billy? Or was it Reynoso?"

"Eh . . ." Andrews watched the man slip his hand to the handle of his revolver. "I don't remember the name. It was the short one."

"That's Billy. Well, the reason Brannon wasn't home is 'cause he's out chasin' down this Andrews fellow. I pity the man that has to go up against Brannon when he's on the prowl."

Andrews faked a smile. "I hear he's quite the shootist. Too bad I didn't get a chance to meet him."

"You're in luck, Hatcher. Brannon's due in here within a couple hours. He knows Andrews, too. He's brought him in before. Wait around and I'll get you properly intro-duced."

"Well, now, I'd like to oblige you . . . but I've got to get to Fort Collins to meet my fiancée."

"Zachariah, I thought you said you just

might forget about her." Sassy stood up, placing her hands on her slightly wide hips.

Andrews smiled from ear to ear.

"It would never work. You're just too exciting of a woman for me. I'm really kind of a boring fellow and —"

"You see? You think some man who's been locked up in Yuma is going to turn me down like that?" Sassy pouted.

"No, ma'am, I don't reckon he would." The deputy grinned. "Well, listen, Hatcher, you take it careful riding north. This Andrews character is a desperate killer. Don't get tangled up with the likes of him."

"No, sir, I won't."

"Is that stew any good?" the shortest of the men asked.

"Well, it depends on how long it's been between meals and whether someone as pretty as Sassy is sittin' at your table. Now I've got to ride. But you men can have my table — or what there is left of it."

"Obliged. Sorry for grillin' ya, Hatcher. We been trailin' this old boy for six days. If Brannon's horse hadn't lamed up, we'd have caught up with him last night."

Andrews stood, picked up his Winchester leaning against the back wall, and walked slowly toward the door.

"Mighty fancy sight you got on that '73," one of the deputies called. "You could pick off a man from seven hundred yards away."

Andrews stiffened. "Or a bull elk from a thousand."

"So you're leavin' me without even a little kiss," Sassy teased, trailing him to the door.

"I don't ever give a pretty woman a *little* kiss!" Andrews winked.

"Prove it!" she insisted.

Andrews threw his arms around the startled girl and leaned her back while pressing his lips into hers. Then suddenly he lifted her back up.

"Whew-eee!" she squealed. "That lucky old Suzy Cedar!"

"Suzanne," Andrews corrected. "She hates to be called Suzy."

He left the cantina without looking back. Tossing the saddlebags over the horn, he mounted the brown horse and rode north.

A good hour later he stopped, glancing over his shoulder. He began to relax.

"Well, Hatcher . . . you saved my skin back there. Thank heavens for dance-hall girls who can't remember one man from another!"

'Course, maybe we do sort of look alike . . . just a tad. If he had been taller, a little more beefed up, and his hair a little longer. I should get mine cut. My old beard probably kept her from telling the difference.

"She don't like to be called Suzy."

Andrews, you started believin' it yourself there for a minute. But you about blew it with that kiss. Too bad that Kentucky woman wouldn't be as easy to fool as Sassy.

Three hours later he camped on the outskirts of a small Utah farm town. Sitting cross-legged next to the fire, he chewed on some dried beef. He kept mulling over the thoughts that had occupied him all afternoon.

If I ride up there, and this Miss Suzanne Cedar thinks I'm Hatcher . . . well . . . maybe I should just string along. I mean I hate to take what another man worked for . . . but Hatcher's dead. And he sure was sorry to disappoint this woman. A remote ranch in Colorado sounds mighty peaceful. Just like startin' life all over. Sort of a new chance. Of course, if someone laid the finger on me . . . but Hatcher said he didn't have any kin. Hardly knew a soul out there, he told me.

Of course, she has a picture — but not a good one. And I've got a beard now . . . but no scar. I'll tell her it healed up.

What did he write in his letters? I know all about her, but nothin' about old Hatcher. She'll see right through me . . . maybe.

But it might be worth a try. I mean, I'll just let it ride. If she thinks I'm Hatcher, I'll go with it and see where it leads. If she takes one look and says, "Who in the world are you?" . . . I'll 'fess up.

"Yep. Hatcher, you can count on me. I'll take care of her. Shoot, she might not be too ugly after all. I once knew a little Baptist girl down in San Diego that could dance up a storm when her pappy wasn't lookin'. Don't you worry about nothin', Zachariah. I'll see that she ain't so disappointed. It's the least I could do for a dyin' man.

"Yes, sir, Mr. Zachariah Hatcher . . . 'it's your misfortune and none of my own.' "

2

September *1882, upper Cache la Poudre River, Colorado.*

Pepper heard the jingle of the bells on the heavy front door of the dance hall and saloon below. She scooted across the bare wooden floor of her upstairs room, flinging a glance in the mirror as she passed by.

"Girls! I need you on the floor!" April Hastings shouted.

Pepper took a second look in the mirror and brushed her blonde curls back on her forehead. Then she ran her fingers across the wrinkles at the corners of her eyes.

Well, girl, you aren't that old! So put on the smile, straighten your dress, don't drink too much, and don't bust his nose when he insults you. Remember to bat your eyes coyly when he says, "Little Lady, you could have been an actress," instead of sayin', "Listen, mister, I'm an actress playing a part every night of the year!"

"Pepper, get down here!" a voice shouted.

Scurrying out of her room, she left the door open. Another girl was at the top of the stairs. The hall smelled of stale smoke and the bitter tinge of liquor.

"Danni Mae, what's all the shoutin' about? Did the army send out another patrol?"

The girl with long, brown hair draped across her back to her waist shot a worried look at Pepper. "There's been an accident. Some people got injured!"

By the time she reached the lower level of the two-story building, Pepper could see April Hastings, most of the girls, and a couple of men standing around the green velvet love seat in the parlor. Several voices fought for control of the conversation. Stack Lowery sat at the piano bench smoking a cigarette, but he had stopped playing.

"What happened?" Pepper asked.

"The pass got washed out last night in the rain storm. Judd hit it straight on. The coach went over the edge!"

"How bad was it?" Pepper asked, still unable to see who was stretched out on the love seat.

"Judd broke his leg, and a couple of men got some cuts and bruises. They're taking some horses and pushing on up to Laramie to get the doctor."

Shouldering her way past Paula and Danni Mae, Pepper glanced down at a woman in a torn dark dress with a bulky, crude bandage wrapped around her head.

"Who's she?"

"A passenger on the stage," one of the men reported.

"She don't look too good. You'd better get her up to Laramie, too."

"Cain't do it. She's too busted up to move," the man replied. "The way she's spittin' blood, she must be busted up on the inside, too."

"You tend to her, Pepper," April Hastings instructed. "These men need to get Judd up the road."

"Tend to her? I ain't no doctor!" Pepper protested.

At times April Hastings had the look of a schoolteacher with fire in her eyes and a ruler in her hand. This was one of those times.

"Pepper, you're the closest thing we got to a doctor for a hundred miles — you and all those home remedies. Now you jist see what you can do. Maybe you can concoct somethin' that will help her be peaceable. 'Member how you helped Stack when he took that knife in the back?"

Pepper Paige, doctor and nurse.

Stack? He's so strong he could recover from fightin' a hundred men with knives.

Those crowded around the injured woman backed away to make room for Pepper.

She looked the injured woman up and

38

down. "Well, darlin', what in the world are you doin' out here? Paula, you bring a basin of water and some towels. At least we can clean her up and see what the problem is."

"Not here," April Hastings insisted. "I'm not runnin' no hospital down here. I've got a business to keep going!"

"Then where?"

"Stack," she shouted to the man at the piano. "Go get a wagon hitched up so they get Judd up to a doctor! Have the men pack the woman up to Pepper's room."

"My room?" Pepper moaned. "You can't put her there!"

"I own this place!" April huffed. "I can put her any place I please! Now take it easy, boys. Don't spill any blood on the divan. That stuff never comes up."

"Wait . . . you can't take her to my room!"

"You take the night off, honey. We ain't goin' to have no one dyin' down here in the dance hall!" April informed her.

"I don't want the night off! Put her in Selena's room. She ain't wantin' to work tonight anyway!"

The dark-skinned Selena Oatley stared with narrow eyes at Pepper. "I ain't never said I didn't want to work tonight!"

"You told me and Danni Mae you were goin' to fake bein' sick just to avoid that rough bunch that's been hangin' around."

"That's a lie, you yellow-haired sow. I ain't never said that!"

"You did too, and you know it, you half-breed!" Pepper hissed.

Instantly, Selena whipped a knife out from under the folds of her dress. "You want to get laid out like this other blonde?" she taunted.

"I ain't afraid of you or that knife," Pepper mocked. "You never done nothin' more serious than pick out splinters with that blade!"

"Pepper," April Hastings injected, "we're taking her to your room. You'll get paid tonight just like the others. Now git your curly head up those stairs. If you two get in another cat fight, one of ya is leavin'. Is that clear?"

"Well, it ain't fair. I can't put little Miss Humpty Dumpty back together again."

"Jist make her comfortable and find out her next of kin," April Hastings instructed. "It's the kind of thing every one of us would want for ourselves."

Hiking up the stairs behind the men carrying the woman, Pepper mumbled, "Pepper, you take care of her. Pepper, you do this. Pepper, you do that. They're covetous. The whole bunch is jealous. I'm the one the boys come here to be with. Beckett and the others don't go chasin' her around the table with their tongues lollin' out.

40

Selena! Hah! She has to stand in line for the leftovers! Sure, let's get Pepper off the floor tonight. She pulls that knife on me again, and I'll take it and slice her. . . ."

"Did you say somethin', ma'am?" one of the men asked.

"It's none of your fat-bellied business!" she barked.

"Oh, well, which is your room?" the startled man stammered.

Pepper looked back over her shoulder to the stairs. "Yeah . . . jist put her in that sloppy room down at the end of the hall," she directed.

Suddenly, a voice boomed from the dance hall floor, "Don't you put her in my room, you Jezebel!"

Pepper turned and stuck out her tongue in the direction of the voice. "Here." She motioned. "This is my room . . . wait! Don't put her on my quilt! Wait! Oh, that's great . . . sure, let her bleed all over my stuff!"

Within moments the men had left, and Pepper stood alone in the small, dark room with her badly injured patient lying on the wood-framed bed. She walked over to the dresser and turned up the lantern. Then she pulled the combs out of her hair and shook the curls down to her shoulder. Slowly she unbuttoned the sleeves of her dress and rolled them up above her elbows as she stared into the mirror.

Pepper, you lucky devil. What a fine life you found for yourself. A magnificent home. A loving family. Surrounded by such close, caring friends! You've got it all, girl. Why, women all over the world would sell their souls to be right here . . . and that's about what it's costin' me!

She reached up as if to brush back a tear . . . but there weren't any.

Picking up the wash basin and a towel, she walked over to the woman on the bed. "Well, darlin', it's time to see what you got."

Pepper spent the next hour cleaning and redressing the severe head wound, tugging off the torn dark dress, and tucking the woman under the covers of her bed. As she did, she could hear noise from downstairs and out in the hallway as business went on as usual for the others.

Without asking, she barefooted her way down to April Hastings's room and dragged the big oak rocking chair back down the hall. Closing the door, she dimmed the lantern, pulled the quilt off the top of the bed, and sat down in the rocker to face the woman. Pepper folded her long, thin legs under her in the chair and wrapped up in the quilt.

"Well, honey," she said to the still unconscious woman, "I don't think you will make it through the night. I surely hope you had a better time of it than me. You got such pretty soft, white skin. Yet you got calluses on your hands. I cain't figure if you are some fancy Eastern city woman or a farm wife who knows how to keep herself.

"Now, look at me, for instance. I've been workin' at jobs like this since I was fifteen. That's almost ten years of smoky rooms, dim lights, vile language, cheatin' card dealers, coarse jokes, and smelly men pawin' at ya. It's life in the shadows, that's what I call it. Others get to live out there in the daylight where everything is bright and beautiful, fresh, and full of promise. We jist live here in the shadows . . . pretendin' to be happy . . . pretendin' to be busy . . . pretendin' our life is leadin' somewhere."

She fell silent for a long moment.

"Well, that's enough about me. Tell me about yourself."

Pepper waited.

There was no answer.

She could still hear the woman's labored breathing.

Pepper leaned her head back on the chair and closed her green eyes. Talking softly, she continued, "Did I tell you I almost got married once? Yeah, I know it's hard to believe, but it's true. About four years ago I was up in Idaho workin' for April. Well, this broad-shouldered straight-shooter came in and chums up to me. He was just the cutest thing I ever saw in my life, you know what I mean? He had a sparkle in his eyes, and I just wanted to melt ever time he smiled at me. Why, the first time he held my hand I thought I'd died and gone to Dixie. His name was Gideon Lane. Now, isn't that a handsome name?

"I suppose you're wonderin' jist what happened? Well, he asked me to marry him. We was goin' to have a big weddin' right there on the north fork of the Clearwater. Everything was all planned for a Saturday weddin' . . . and then I woke up Wednesday mornin', saddled me pony, and rode off.

"Yep . . . I rode away without sayin' a word. Missy, I jist couldn't do it. I've never had much of a family, and I suddenly realized I didn't have any idea in the world about how to be a wife. It scared me to death. Gideon deserved somethin' better than me, that's for sure. I worked down in Boise City until April decided to open up in Colorado, and she gave me this job. You got a mighty pretty ring on your hand. You must be quite a charmer . . . but you shouldn't pin up that beautiful hair. Us blondes has got a divine right to flaunt our hair, don't you think so?"

There was no answer from the woman.

About midnight the lantern flickered out.

At 2:00 A.M. the activities downstairs began to wind down.

At 3:00 A.M. April Hastings opened the door and, holding a lantern in her hand, peeked in. "Pepper, now what are you doin' in bed? . . . Oh, there you are! You know, that gal sort of looks like you — in the shadows. I thought it was you under them covers. Is she still alive?"

"Yeah. But she hasn't woke up or said anythin'."

"Here's her valise." April Hastings set a leather case inside the door. "I guess she left several trunks at the Wemberly House in Fort Collins. At least, that's what Judd reported."

"Where was she going?" Pepper asked.

"Don't rightly know. She told Judd she was expecting to meet some man out here somewhere."

"Well, I don't think she'll make it," Pepper observed. "I got your rocking chair."

"I figured as much. I'll see you in the mornin'." April Hastings turned and closed the door behind her, leaving Pepper once more with the injured woman.

Scooting through the dark, Pepper re-lit the lantern and toted the leather case back to the rocking chair.

"Honey, maybe there's some clue to who you are in here. So I hope you don't mind me snooping around. Well, now, ain't that fancy? Everything organized in neat little velvet bags.

"Cosmetics . . . I didn't know you used them. And some fancy perfume? Ooohweee, honey, if that don't trap the men, nothin' will! Good grief, girl, where did you get all this money? You ain't a bank robber, are you? A Bible? Let me see . . . it must be in the front. Here it is. Miss Suzanne Cedar, born June 1858, Franklin County, Kentucky. Father: Thaddeus S. Cedar. Mother: Mavis Liddon Cedar. Brother: Abel Giles Cedar.

"Well, Miss Cedar, that tells who you are, but not why you're out in the mountains of Colorado. You're about my age, but I don't think I look nothin' like you. April has probably been drinkin'."

She continued digging in the valise.

"Would you look at these pretties! Suzanne! A Bible-readin' girl like you shouldn't be wearin' . . . letters? These must be real important. You've almost worn the ink off them. You got them numbered on the outside.

"Number 1. 'February 23, 1881. Dear Miss Suzanne Cedar.' Who is this guy? He doesn't even know you . . . oh, knows your brother, Abel. Let's see, he wanted to write to the golden-haired sister. Honey, he's buttering you up for something.

"Ah, he's medium height and build, dark hair, brown eyes. 1848? Suzanne, this man's ten years older than you. Punchin'

46

cows . . . goin' to drive a herd to Montana and then buy a ranch and settle down. Oh, brother, is he out shoppin' for a wife? . . . Zachariah M. Hatcher. That's a handsome name. A man like that could be governor some day.

"Number 2. She must have wrote back to him. He says the ranch has a good-sized house and barn. That's it, honey, this old boy's lookin' for someone to milk the cows. You didn't string along with this, did you? 'I'm drawn irresistibly once again to stay in this land, a land too vast to describe.' Oh, you're gettin' suckered, Suzanne Cedar.

"Number 3. He pushed the cattle through . . . tough times . . . He's a Presbyterian . . . doesn't drink? Sure, Suzanne, don't fall for it. They all make wild promises. He's got few friends . . . family's died . . . 'can only speak to you.' Oh, brother, get out the violins! She's a singer? A patient lady? You can say that again, Mr. Hatcher. I would have dumped you a long time ago!"

Pepper dragged her rocking chair over closer to the lantern, turned up the wick, and sat back down to read letter number 4.

"He bought the ranch . . . still trying to butter her up . . . doesn't have any cows. What good is a ranch without cows? He wears a .44 but hasn't shot anyone. He sent a photograph."

She dug through the valise, but she

found no photograph.

"Number 5. 'Dear Suzanne.' Now he's gettin' real chummy. He's headed to Arizona to look for her brother and buy some bulls. Honey, the whole thing smells like bull. Let's see, the ranch is on the western slope of the Medicine Bows by the Camp, Village Belle, and Lawrence Creeks. The Triple Creek Ranch? That makes sense. Five thousand acres . . . That's a nice start. Big, wood-frame house with immense fireplace, small kitchen, one bedroom. But the barn is in good condition. Well, whoop-te-do, Mr. Hatcher! . . . an engagement ring. He sent a ring through the mail without meeting you? 'Frightfully bold . . .' Boy, ain't that the truth?"

Pepper pulled the blanket up over her shoulders and then continued scanning the letters.

"Number 6. Condolences and prayers? Oh, your father died. . . . You could bring your Kentucky horses. That's why you have calluses, darlin'. . . . 'Every beautiful sunset, every crisp clear mountain morning, every smile in a child's face makes me long to share these experiences with you.' "

Pepper stared over at the injured woman on the bed. Then she reached up to wipe her eyes.

But there were no tears.

"Number 7. He's in Arizona now . . .

worries that the photograph wasn't a good likeness of him . . . oh, that's great! Will meet you in Fort Collins sometime around the nineteenth of September. That was last Monday! 'Are we really going to get to meet? To look into each others eyes? To touch?' "

She glanced again at the woman in the bed, who seemed to be struggling for every breath. "Don't count on seeing or touching her, Mr. Zachariah Hatcher. Your lady ain't doin' so well."

"Number 8. Boy, this is a short one. Let's see . . . got her letter . . . leaving Arizona for the ranch. It's about one hundred miles from Fort Collins. He might be late, but he will be coming in on the Cache la Poudre River Road. Hopes to be there by the twenty-second. That's why she's here! That was yesterday. She's going out to the ranch."

Pepper set the valise on the floor and turned the lantern off. She rubbed her stiff shoulders and then pulled the quilt up tight around her neck.

"It's cold in here," she murmured. "It's gettin' real cold."

She fell asleep dreaming of a big house with a huge rock fireplace.

Startled awake, Pepper could feel the neck of her still-buttoned collar filled with sweat. She heard a voice and pushed

49

the blanket down.

The voice was so faint it was almost a whisper.

"Zachariah?"

"Miss Cedar?" Pepper spoke softly.

"Yes . . . yes! Who is it? Where am I? I can't see anything."

"I'll light a lantern."

"Where am I? My chest . . . Is there something lying on my chest?"

"No, ma'am, just a blanket." Pepper lit the lantern, turned it up, and walked over to the bedside.

"Now then, I'm Aimee Paige, but most of the girls here call me Pepper and —"

"The lantern . . . Are you going to turn on the lantern?"

"The lantern is lit. It's sitting over there . . . oh!" she gasped.

"I can't see!" Suzanne moaned. I can't see!"

Pepper reached out with a damp cloth and stroked the woman's battered forehead. "Just relax. You've been in a bad stagecoach accident. Your vision will probably be back by morning."

"Is this a hospital?" Miss Cedar inquired.

"Well, you might call it that."

"Are you a nurse?"

"Eh . . . yeah . . . that's right. I'm your nurse, Miss Cedar."

"How do you know my name?"

Pepper brought her hand back to her lap. "Oh . . . I, eh, I mean, the men who brought you in told me that."

"How did they know? I didn't tell anyone my name since I arrived in Colorado."

"Oh . . . well, you know men. A beautiful blonde lady like yourself comes into the region. One of them will scout around and find out your name."

For several minutes there was silence.

"Thank you for the compliment," Cedar finally offered. "I'm sure I'm not much of a beauty right now."

"Well, I don't think Mr. Zachariah Hatcher would mind one bit."

"Zach . . . oh, Zach! Do you know him? Why can't I get my breath? Are you sure there's nothing mashing my chest down?"

"Just a blanket. I'll move it. Is that better?"

"Do you know Zach? We're going to get married."

"Well, Miss Cedar . . . eh . . . sure! Everyone knows Zachariah Hatcher. Why, he's a big-time cattle rancher in these parts. He owns that Triple Creek Ranch."

"Yes, that's him! Are we very far from the ranch?"

"Well, I'm not real good on distances, but I reckon it's another seventy miles or so."

"And you still know him?"

"Oh, sure."

"But I thought he didn't have many friends up here."

"Well . . . he's just modest, you know what I mean?"

"Tell me about him."

"You mean what he looks like?"

"Yes . . . and about his personality, his character."

"Eh," Pepper stammered, "well . . . where should I begin? Let's see . . . He's about medium height, medium build, dark hair —"

"Dark brown?"

"Yeah, but you know those cattlemen. He always has his Stetson on. I hope I'm not steppin' out of line, Miss Cedar, but he really is a handsome man."

"That's just the way I imagined him." Suzanne Cedar drew each breath slowly. "Listen, Miss Paige . . . Can I call you Aimee?"

"Just call me Pepper. I wouldn't know how to respond if anyone called me something else."

"All right, Pepper. My, that is an unusual name for a nurse. Anyway . . . tell me, what is Mr. Hatcher like?"

"Well, now, I can tell you this. I've been in this country for four years, and I ain't never heard one mean word about Zachariah Hatcher."

"He seems to be a very kind and sensitive

man," Cedar offered.

"You took the words right out of my mouth."

"Pepper . . . that heaviness is back on my chest . . . Are you pushing me? It's cold. Is there a window open? I feel the snow . . . Is that snow?"

Pepper Paige moved closer to the woman on the bed. She noticed Suzanne Cedar's eyes stared blankly toward the ceiling. Her color was nearly the same as the gray flannel sheets. Pepper pulled the blankets up around Suzanne's neck, took hold of her hand, and rested the other one on her forehead.

"Pepper?"

"I'm here."

"I'm not going . . . to live to see Mr. Hatcher, am I?"

"No, ma'am . . . I don't believe you will."

"My heart breaks."

"I know you're hurtin' real bad. I wish I could do somethin'."

"I'm ready for my Jesus. I mean, my heart breaks when I think of the disappointment and grief for Zach." She gasped at the pain. "I should never have come out here. I was afraid I wasn't sturdy enough. I didn't even last three days."

"Well, I suppose . . . eh, you know . . ." Pepper stumbled with the words. "I guess the good Lord has our days numbered."

"Yes, perhaps."

She was silent for several minutes.

"Pepper? Are you still there?" she whispered.

"I'm here, darlin'."

"You'll tell him, won't you?"

"Mr. Hatcher?"

"Yes . . . please tell him I loved him with all my heart. Tell him, please!"

Pepper Paige took a deep breath and wiped her eyes.

There were no tears.

"I'll tell him. You can count on it."

"You know what, Pepper? I think you might be an angel."

"A what?"

"I think you're an angel the Lord sent just to help me now."

"Nobody ever called me an angel unless he was tryin' to get me to give him somethin'."

"What do you . . . look like?"

"I look a lot like you. About your age, blonde hair. I even have green eyes. 'Course, you look like a beautiful porcelain doll that's been kept on the shelf. Me — I look like an old gunny sack doll that's been tied to a rope and drug behind a wagon, if you know what I mean."

The woman in the bed began to groan at every breath. "I can't take this pain anymore, Pepper," she gasped.

"Miss Cedar, I'm terrible sorry, but we

don't have any laudanum. I can go get you some whiskey if you'd like."

"No . . . no . . . it's just . . . it hurts so much!"

"Maybe . . . eh . . . well, maybe it's just time to let go. I can guarantee that Heaven's got to be a better place than this."

"Pepper . . . pray for me!"

"I . . . ma'am . . . I jist . . . I don't know how."

"Lord," Suzanne Cedar whispered, "take good care of my Zachariah . . . and give a special blessing to my angel, Pepper. I don't know what I would . . . what . . . I don't . . . alone . . . oh, Pepper!"

It was all over.

No more pain on the face.

No struggle for breath.

No more pressure on the chest.

No more cold wind.

No more anxiety over a lover she had never met.

Pepper folded Suzanne Cedar's arms on her chest and pulled the flannel sheet over her head.

"Good-bye, darlin'. It would have been nice to have more time to visit. But we didn't exactly travel in the same circles."

Pepper reached up and dabbed at dry, dry eyes.

At daylight Pepper, draped in her robe,

shuffled down the wooden stairs barefoot and across the sticky floor of the main room. Within minutes she had the wood stove in the kitchen stoked and water beginning to warm. The coffee was ready by the time Danni Mae Walters came in wearing a long flannel gown and red satin lace-up boots.

"You gettin' up or goin' to bed?" Pepper asked her.

"Oh? I just was too tired to pull my boots off. How's your patient? Still hurtin'?"

"No pain this mornin'."

"She goin' to pull through?"

"She's dead."

Danni Mae poured herself a cup of coffee, pulled up a wooden chair next to Pepper's, and plopped down.

"It don't figure, does it?" she finally muttered.

"Nope. She was a proper lady from back East. Been out here three days, and she's dead. How many gunfights you figure there've been in this dance hall since we came here, Danni Mae?"

"Gunfights? About fifty, I suppose."

"And how many knifings?"

"Twice that amount."

"And how many head-bustin' fist fights?"

"Are you kidding? Who in the world could count those?"

"We live through it all."

56

"Well, that's one positive thing you can say about it."

"And we got nothin' when we're through! Our life is preserved so we can go on gettin' nothin'. But Suzanne Cedar, she —"

"Who?"

"That dead lady up in my room. We was visitin' a little last night. She had everything to live for. A rancher who wanted to marry her, a nice home, a future. But she's dead, and we're alive. It just don't add up."

"Add up or not, personally I'm glad it's not me lyin' dead up there." Danni Mae shrugged.

"When you get tired of doin' this, what will you do, Danni Mae?"

"Marry some cowboy, I guess . . . I don't know. I just sort of take it one day at a time. Speakin' of stabbin's, Selena's still threatenin' to knife you."

"I'm goin' to take that sticker from her and cut off that black hair if she doesn't calm down!"

"Watch out for her, Pepper. I hear she got run out of Central City for stabbing one of the girls."

"Danni Mae, nobody ever got run out of Central City for knifin' someone. But they might have got carried out in a box. I'll watch out for her."

"What you goin' to do with that body in your room?" Danni Mae held out the front of her gown and fanned it back and forth. She stood up and refilled the two coffee cups and then pulled her chair back away from the wood stove.

"I guess I'll get Stack to help me bury her out back. Then I'll send a letter to her mama. If I can find an address."

"Well, Stack might be late gettin' around. He had a run-in with Jordan Beckett last night. Several of Beckett's boys tried workin' him over."

"Beckett was here?"

"Yep."

"Drunk?"

"Yep."

"He's a jerk."

"And he was lookin' for you. That's what made him so obnoxious. He wanted to promenade with his 'golden-haired princess.' He insisted that you were standin' him up. You know how mean he gets when he's been drinkin'. It's all Stack could do to keep him from bustin' upstairs."

"I'm glad I missed him."

"Oh, he'll be back. April told him you'd be back on the floor tonight. And he's threatenin' to shoot any man who gets between you and him."

"Yeah . . . that certainly gives me something to look forward to. Look, Danni Mae, I'm going to take this hot water upstairs and have a sponge bath. If you see Stack, tell him to build us a pine box and dig out the shovels."

"Someday it will be me and you up there under a scrawny cedar, Pepper."

"Not in a dump like this."

"Sure . . . I can think of a lot of places worse than this one." Danni Mae shrugged.

"That's where you got me beat." Pepper scooted toward the doorless entry. "I can't think of many places more depressing than this."

"Girl, you sure got a bad case of the sours!"

"I think I'm just tired," Pepper called back toward the kitchen. "Real tired."

Stack Lowery and a boy named Johnny had dug a hole up on Pingree Hill and left a pine box in the hallway when Pepper finally exited her room dressed for the day.

Pepper dragged the box into her room and scooted it over by the bed.

"Honey, we'll just put you out on the mountain until your kin claims ya. It's the best we got out here. You were travelin' mighty light on dresses. I suppose they're back at Fort Collins with your baggage. Well, I want you to look nice. Now I know you ain't never worn a dress like this green satin, but I want you to be buried in it."

It took her a good hour to pull the dress onto the body of Suzanne Cedar, wrap her in an old quilt, and lay her in the pine box. She was nailing the lid down when Stack Lowery appeared at the door.

"Miss Pepper? You ready for me and Johnny to put her under?"

"Yeah . . . I'll go with ya," Pepper announced as she picked up a black Bible from the dresser.

"You goin' to read over her?" Stack asked.

"Yeah, I guess."

"Well, a man learns somethin' new ever' day. I never knowed you had a Bible."

"It belongs to her. It just seems like the right thing to do."

"Yes, ma'am, it surely does."

Hardly anyone talked about the death of Suzanne Cedar that night as a crowd started to belly up to the bar and then stagger out to the dance floor. Pepper's feet were already tired when Jordan Beckett walked in and headed straight for her.

"Well, here's my golden-haired, green-eyed darlin'!" he blustered. "Why did you hide from me last night?"

"Let's just say I was sittin' up with a very sick friend."

"Yeah, sure. And did she have a miraculous recovery tonight?"

"Nope. She died."

"And I say you was jist tryin' to dodge me." He grabbed her arm tight, and pain shot up to the shoulder. "You and me is goin' out behind the barn for a little private talk!"

"Beckett, I do believe you're the most egotistical, cold-hearted, foul-mouthed, repulsive, tobacco-chewin' jerk in the state of Colorado. There isn't a lady on the face of the earth who would walk out behind the barn with you!"

The big man's face flushed red.

"I ain't talkin' to no lady. I'm talkin' to you, Pepper Paige! I paid my money, and I get my choice. You're it!" he hollered.

At great pain, she pulled her arm free and turned her back on Beckett. Everyone had stopped to watch the two of them. Stack Lowery stopped playing the piano and started working his way through the crowd toward her.

"It ain't goin' to work. I ain't leavin', and there's no one here who can stop me!" he shouted.

She noticed that Stack was held at bay by two of Beckett's men who pointed carbines.

"You see, Angel, this is your lucky night!"

"What did you call me?"

"Angel. I called you Angel. Why?"

"Come here!" she commanded and slipped her arms around his black leather vest as he stepped closer, hugging him close.

"Ya see, boys, you jist got to know how

to treat them. Now that's better, Angel —"

Pepper had Beckett's gun out of its holster and jammed the weapon, fully cocked, into his ear.

"You listen, and you listen good. There ain't no one left on this earth who gets to call me Angel. You got that? Now you turn around and walk out that door. Don't you ever, ever lay your filthy hands on me again," she yelled.

"You can't treat me this way," he blustered. "You can't treat me this way! You'll pay for this!"

She jammed the revolver, still cocked, down the front of his trousers behind his belt. "You better thank your lucky stars that I didn't pull the trigger," she said with a sneer. Then she turned around and scooted up the stairs to her room.

She could hear the room fill with shouts and laughter. It would not be long, she knew, before she would have a visit from April.

Upon closing the door, she immediately noticed that Suzanne Cedar's valise was missing. Kicking open the door at the end of the hall, she found a surprised Selena Oatley digging through the leather bag.

"Gimme that!" Pepper barked.

"It ain't yours," Selena insisted. "I got as much right to it as you do."

"You got no rights at all! I'm turnin' it all

over to her fiancé!" Pepper wrenched the bag away from the dark-haired girl.

Suddenly Selena pulled out her knife and waved it at Pepper. 'You ain't gettin' nothing but the sharp end of a steel blade!" she hissed.

Holding the handle, Pepper whirled the leather bag at Selena's extended arm, knocking the knife to the far wall. Selena took a wild swing, but Pepper ducked and caught the other girl with a doubled-up fist to the stomach and another quick jab to the chin. Selena sprawled across her bed.

Pepper glanced into the bag and flipped through the contents that had been poured out of the little velvet bags.

"Where's the cash, Selena?" she demanded.

"Weren't no cash in there," Selena lied. Suddenly she lunged toward the knife. Pepper locked her left arm around Selena's neck, shoved her free hand down the decollete bodice of the other girl's dress, and yanked out a wad of bills.

"My, look what I found!" She shoved the money into the leather suitcase and twirled back out into the hall.

"I'll kill you. You — you witch!" Selena jeered.

"Not in my house!" April Hastings boomed.

"Pepper, I've just about had it with you

tonight. You know I can't keep a girl who insults the customers and abuses the other girls. Now get down there and apologize to Beckett. I can't afford to lose the business of that whole bunch."

"April . . . I ain't goin' to apologize!"

"You most certainly are! Now I told you to —"

"You aren't tellin' me nothin' — ever again!" Pepper screamed. "I quit!"

"Then you'll be out of that room by breakfast," April hollered.

"It will be a delight!" Pepper slammed and locked the door to her room.

She spent the night in the rocking chair, facing the door, with a blanket wrapped around her, a Remington .41 rimfire, pearl-handled pocket revolver clasped in one hand and the leather valise in her lap.

During the long night she re-read the letters from Zachariah Hatcher several times and examined every item as she carefully put them back in the velvet bags. At daylight she was packed, dressed, and waiting when Stack Lowery came to her door.

"Miss Pepper? You need a ride somewhere? I'm headin' out to buy some supplies."

"You goin' east or west?"

"West, I reckon. The pass is still washed

out toward the east."

"I'll ride with you for a while. I've got to find some rancher over there."

With both her suitcase and Suzanne Cedar's valise in the wagon, Pepper hugged Danni Mae Walters, Paula St. Lucie, and Nevada Young. She nodded at April Hastings who sat passively on the porch of her establishment. Selena Oatley was not in sight.

"Can you drive up there by that grave, Stack?"

"I reckon so."

When the two-horse wagon reached the grave site, he stopped the team. "You gettin' out?"

"Nope. I just needed to say somethin'." She looked down at the fresh dirt and sighed.

Well, darlin' . . . you yourself said that Mr. Zachariah Hatcher deserved to be greeted by his fiancée, and I'm goin' to see that he is. Now you know I ain't stealin' your man, cause, well, you never had him, and besides you're up there frolickin' past them pearly gates. Maybe he won't know the difference between one green-eyed blonde and another.

She reached up and wiped her eyes. There were no tears.

3

Tap Andrews ranged up through Utah, across the northwest corner of Colorado, arriving at the North Platte River on September 21, 1882. He turned east, crossed the Michigan River, and rode into a small settlement called McCurley.

He made a few inquiries, bought a short black horse, extra saddle, and as many groceries as he could carry on the horse. Then he headed on north on a trail that took him past Sentinel Mountain to Pinkham Creek. From there he turned due west and began the ascent to Lawrence Creek.

Finally he stopped at the base of a deep canyon to rest the horses. He rolled his jacket and tied it behind the cantle. Pulling a piece of jerky out of his brown deerskin vest pocket, he surveyed the countryside.

"Well, ponies, this is our new home. This country just begs for cows. Mountains, valleys, streams, thick grass . . . Oh, sure it's all brown now, but can you imagine how it looks in the spring? . . . And we'll have plenty of privacy! We haven't seen a house or fresh wagon rut for twenty miles. Arizona bounty hunters will never come up here. No wonder Hatcher bought this place!"

He walked the horses up the trail for a couple of miles. Then he tightened the latigo, swung back into the well-worn saddle, and rode straight up the creek until he spotted a wood-frame house and huge barn tucked back against a bluff of the Medicine Bow Mountains. About a half-mile away flowed a slowly moving stream.

At least, I think this is Hatcher's place. It looks deserted enough.

Stopping the horses, he soaked up the view. He took a deep breath and sighed.

"Brownie, I just didn't know there were still places like this around. I mean, I always hoped there was . . . I always pretended that someday I'd quit driftin' and buy me a spread like this. But sometimes . . . well, I just got to thinkin' a place like this didn't exist anymore."

He stopped and tied off both horses to a post in the midst of a packed-dirt yard.

"Well, boys, you wait out here, and I'll check the place. I'm not sure Hatcher had time to fix it up for company . . . . I'm not even sure he's been here. That old boy down at McCurley's store and hotel sure didn't bat an eye when I told him I was Zach Hatcher."

As he walked across the wooden porch, he heard the rattle of pans inside the house.

Someone's home! Maybe this isn't Hatcher's place! I could have got it all wrong . . . or maybe he has a cook . . . or hired hands.

Staying on the left side of the doorway so that he would be hidden from anyone swinging the door open, he pounded on the heavy oak and shouted, "Ho! In the house! Anyone home?"

There was no answer.

He banged and shouted again, *"¡Hola! En la casa! ¿Quién es usted?"*

There was still no answer.

Andrews drew his Colt out of the holster, but he changed his mind about cocking it.

"Look, I heard you in there . . . Now I've got to talk to you! Does the name Zachariah Hatcher mean anything to you?"

Pans crashed.

"Look, I'm comin' in now, and I have my gun drawn. All I want to do is talk, *comprende?"*

With a .44 Colt in his right hand, Andrews lifted the latch on the door and slowly swung it open. The hinges squealed loudly, and the stillness of the house seemed to amplify the sound. The air smelled musty and tinged with old smoke. The room was big but had few furnishings. It looked like no one had been there for weeks.

"Hello! Anyone home?" he called. Still carrying his drawn Colt, he stepped lightly toward a back room. A rough pine four-poster bed was up against a window, with a long dresser built right into the wall.

"Hello!" he called. Andrews slapped the bed covers, and dust fogged the room. Gently he walked back out into the big room and then around into the kitchen. Cupboards stretched from floor to ceiling. He found a newer looking cookstove on the far wall, a six-foot-square butcher's block in the very center of the room, and a pantry without a door on the left side. A couple of pans littered the floor. A back door on the far wall seemed to lead outside. The door was propped open several inches with an old boot.

"What in the world?" Andrews mumbled. "Hatcher left the door open on purpose?"

Sensing movement to the right, he whirled and pointed his .44. Tap Andrews found himself staring into the slitted eyes of a huge gray and white cat sitting on the counter with its front paws tucked under its shoulders.

"A cat? What are you doin' here?"

The cat stared.

"So Hatcher has a cat? And he left the back door propped so you could go and come as you please. Well, come here!"

He reached over and scooped up the cat, which seemed content to stay in his rough, callused hands.

"Well, boy, what's your name? I mean, what will I call you? I suppose I should know your name. If Hatcher told Miss Cedar your name . . . I'll wait until she mentions your name."

"But why a cat? Way out here?"

A dark shadow raced across the kitchen floor, and the cat sprang out of his arms, claws protracted. Within seconds the feline returned from behind the butcher block with a mouse clutched in its teeth. The gray and white cat scurried out the back door and into the yard.

"A little dinner outside? You proved your point. We can use a mouser. But no eatin' in the kitchen, you understand?"

He turned back to the big front room. Well, it surely doesn't look like anyone's been here — not even that Cedar woman."

He opened all the shutters and windows that weren't stuck and propped both the front and back doors open.

"That ought to air it out . . . Come on, ponies, let's see what your house looks like."

Andrews led the animals to the huge barn next to some stout corrals. The tall gable-roofed structure smelled of dried manure and old hay. It was clean, neat, and looked as if it had been used more recently than the house.

"Well, would you look at this, boys! She's

a beaut! Clean stalls, plenty of hay upstairs — although it looks like last year's crop — and a water pump right in the barn!"

Within a few minutes he had the horses stripped down, rubbed off, watered, and placed in a stall with some hay. He was surprised that the leathers in the pump had not dried out and cracked.

He carried the supplies to the house, hunted for a broom, and began to clean up. With every sweep of the broom, dust fogged the room, but a slight breeze began to clear the air. He hung the bedding on the corral fence and beat it with the broom. Then he tossed the mattress on the roof of the front porch.

This might be a big waste of time. But I'll enjoy it for one night at least. Then I'll head down the road and see if I can find Miss Suzanne Cedar. I surely would like this to work out. With the right woman at his side, a man could sit up and watch the rest of the world go on by.

He was scooting a big chunk of split red fir into the crackling fire when he heard riders approach. Instantly, he grabbed up his Winchester, cocked it, and then stepped to the open doorway. Two punchers rode into the yard from the north, circled between the barn and the house, and then drew up at the hitching post.

If these boys knew Zachariah Hatcher, I'll

have a lot of explainin' to do. Well, Tap, here's a good test.

He set his Winchester in the doorway and walked toward the men. "Evenin', fellas!" he called. "What can I do for you?"

"Are you Hatcher?" the taller of the two asked.

"Well, that's what folks have been calling me. Boys, come on down and sit a spell. The coffee's not hot yet, but I got the water warmin'."

"Thank ya, we appreciate it." The short one in the black shirt nodded, loosening his red bandanna and shaking out the dust.

Walking with them back to the house, Andrews asked, "Can I do anything for ya?"

"Well, sir . . . Mr. Hatcher . . . we is just sort of wanting to welcome you to the neighborhood. My name's Wiley, and this here's Quail."

"You take to sleeping on the roof?" Quail motioned to the mattress on the shingled roof of the front porch.

"I just got this place, and it needs freshin' up. I figured a little air and sunlight would do it good."

"We're a bit dirty for house visitin'," Wiley offered. "Maybe we ought to drink that coffee out here."

"Boys, do you work for an outfit around here?"

"Yes, sir."

"Well, let me tell you somethin' right up front. Punchers are welcome inside my house any day of the week, you understand?"

"Thank ya, that's right neighborly."

"Bankers, on the other hand, don't get further than that scrub cedar down the road. Now make yourself at home, and we'll wait for that coffee to boil."

"Mr. Hatcher, we came down —"

"Now, Wiley, I don't much cotton to being called Mr. Hatcher. You can call me Zach. Or just use my nickname — Tap."

"Tap?"

"As in tapadera."

"Yes, sir . . . well, Tap, we work up across the state line on the Rafter R Ranch. We were ridin' the drift line and thought we'd come down and introduce ourselves. We'll surely try to keep the Wyoming beef off your range. Sometimes in the blizzards, they wander down this way. They'll all be branded Rafter R."

"Well, it's going to take me a while to build the place up," Tap offered. "I hope to have several hundred head running by early next summer."

"What's your brand goin' to be?"

Brand? I don't even know if I'll be here tomorrow.

"Well, I'm thinkin' of making it the . . . Triple Creek Ranch. So I'll burn a TC with a wavy line underneath. Is that going to look too much like any others around here?"

"Nope. Don't think so."

Quail stood up and walked over to the coffeepot which hung on an iron hook at the front of the fireplace. He poured himself a cup of coffee and turned back to Andrews. Steam rose from the blue enameled tin cup, and he waved it under his chin to enjoy the full aroma.

"Now, there's one other thing you ought to know."

"What's that?"

"Well, the big augur up on Rafter R is a fellow named Fightin' Ed Casey. You ever heard of him?"

"Nope. But I presume he got his name honestly."

"You're right about that." Wiley nodded. He had his eyes on buying this place himself, so he don't intend on being real neighborly. He won't take too kindly to your coming over the line lookin' for strays and the like. But you won't get no trouble from us. We jist thought it fair to warn you."

"You see," put in Quail, "the old boy who had this place last was a, well, a little careless about his friends. Some say a band of rustlers and bank thieves were campin' in here. So Casey felt he needed to have control down here too."

74

"And if he gets liquored up," Quail added, he'll pull a gun to get his way." He downed his coffee and walked toward the door. "We'd better be headin' back."

"You boys are welcome to stay for supper. Can't promise it will be too fancy."

"No, sir . . . eh, Tap, it will be after dark before we make camp as it is. But we surely do thank you for the welcome."

They all hiked back out to the yard.

"Water up those ponies and grab a little hay from the barn," Tap offered.

"Thank ya, we'll do that. Say, you've spent a little time pushing someone else's cattle, haven't ya?"

"Many a long, long day, boys." Andrews nodded. "Now whenever you need to come this way, you boys plan on puttin' up with us. There isn't room in the house, but you can always camp out in the barn, whether we're home or not."

"We? You got family, Tap?" Quail asked as he mounted the gray horse.

"Not yet. But I'm seriously thinkin' of takin' a wife."

"Oh, that's fine . . . mighty fine." Wiley smiled. "And if you throw a big dance, be sure and send us up an invite."

"I'll do it, boys." Tap smiled. "And thanks for the visit."

Within a few minutes they left the barn, waved at Tap who was tugging the mattress off the porch roof, and rode north.

Well, they certainly think I'm Hatcher. I hope Miss Suzanne Cedar from Kentucky is as easy to fool, 'cause I sure am startin' to like this place.

That evening Andrews checked on the horses, examined the corrals — which he found in good shape, cooked himself a little supper, trimmed up the four lanterns he found in working condition, and fed the cat some scraps. She then took up residence in front of the fireplace.

By the time the sun sank behind Pinkham Mountain, Tap had washed up and flopped into a chair he had dragged out on the front porch of the ranch house. He sat staring to the south. The hot coffee from the thick porcelain cup, which had a chip out of the handle, steamed his still unshaven face.

"You know, Hatcher, no wonder you hated dyin'. Heaven can't be a whole lot better than this. And that other place — the one down below — it's got to be just about the opposite of this ranch. No matter what Miss Suzanne Cedar looks like, you have yourself a gold mine of contentment.

"This is all I ever wanted. Just a place to take care of, an operation that pays the food bills. Some place out of the way, where I'm free to laugh and love and raise a family. A place where no one tries to run my life."

Leaning back in the chair, he noticed the gray and white cat had come out the partially open door. He patted his lap, and the cat immediately jumped up and settled down.

"Now look, cat. I don't have much use for your type, so you'll have to toe the line," Andrews instructed as he petted long strokes down the animal's back. "And I can't name you until Miss Suzanne gets here. I don't want cat hair spread all over my house, or you'll be living out there with Brownie and Onespot. Now, have you got all that?"

The cat answered with a purr.

That's what every man wants. A quiet place of his own. That's what drove Daddy to the gold fields of Tuolumne Creek in '49. He was goin' to make it big and then settle down. That's all Mama, bless her métis soul, ever wanted. She followed Daddy to every gold and silver camp in three counties. She would have loved to come out on this porch and just sit. That's what Stoddard was after. Three more years in the army, and then he would have retired. But the Second Cavalry, D Troop, fought at Rosebud with General Crook, and he took it full in that handsome face of his. Maybe someday down the line, I could bring his remains down here and bury him on this mountain.

Tap Andrews — the cowboy . . . the gambler . . . the saloon owner . . . the hired gun . . . the ladies' man — this is all he ever wanted. Yeah, that old boy at Mexican Wells called me a ladies' man. All I ever wanted was one to settle down with, but I never had anything to offer her. A man's got to have something to bring her home to.

I could make her a good husband. I really could. But she deserves something better than a lyin' drifter. Tap, she wouldn't give you the time of day if she knew who you really are. Your type's down there in the cantina at Mexican Wells.

Shoot, maybe Miss Cedar will sell me the ranch. But I don't have any money. Maybe she'll go back east and let me run the place. Then I'll ride back down to Arizona and find a wife and . . . no. I can't go back!

This is it.

This is my one chance.

I don't plan on missin' it. Miss Cedar, you're expecting a fine, upstandin' Christian gentleman rancher, and that's exactly what you're goin' to get.

Sittin' on my porch. Enjoyin' the sunset. I do believe this is why we were created.

"You know, cat, by tomorrow this dream might all be smoke, but I am going to enjoy it tonight."

Until it got too dark to see, Tap cleaned his rifle and his revolver. With a buckhorn folding knife, he scraped a dozen brass casings clean and carefully reloaded the shells. His bullet belt was filled when he re-entered the house.

That night Andrews lay in bed reading Zachariah Hatcher's Bible. He started out trying to memorize the whole Hatcher family, whose names were inscribed on the first few pages. Then he began to scan the text and read a few of the verses Hatcher had marked.

Finally, he carefully laid the Bible on the long dresser and turned off the lantern. Moonlight filtered through the curtainless window.

"Well, Andrews, if she quizzes you about the Bible, you're in big trouble!"

He cocked the Winchester '73, set the hammer on safety, and leaned it against the log wall by the headboard. Then he hung his holster and bullet belt on the bedpost. He pulled out the Colt, opened the cylinder, slipped one more .44-40 into the sixth chamber, and dropped it back into the holster. He crawled under the covers, lay on his back, scrunched the worn-down pillow under his head, and instantly went to sleep.

Stack Lowery was not noted as a conversationalist. He had the unusual dual talents of playing the piano and throwing drunks out of saloons owned by April Hastings. Pepper and the other girls knew he was the only man alive who would literally die to protect them. Stack was every girl's loyal brother. It was well into afternoon before Pepper got him started talking.

"You know, Stack, this sure is beautiful country out here, isn't it? Just look down there at that valley! Why, some big old ranch house would make it sort of look like Heaven. You know what I love about this country? It's big and fresh and clean. Sometimes I feel kind of dirty out in the open . . . like I better scrub up, or they won't let me live here."

"Where you going to go, Miss Pepper?" Stack asked. "I sure hate to see you leave Miss April. Maybe you could go back and talk to her. You and her's been together for an awful long time. She's more reasonable in the mornin', you know."

"Stack . . . I want something better than that dance hall. All of us do. Me, Danni Mae, Nevada, Paula, even Selena. It was supposed to be a place to work until something else came along. Well, nothin' came. Not eight years ago, not this year. So I'm goin' to find somethin' else."

"I hear Bob McCurley got his place open near the North Platte. I'm going right by there. I did him a favor last spring. I could

80

ask him to give you a job."

"I'm not workin' in any more saloons or dance halls. I'm not goin' to do it. I knew it last night with Jordan Beckett. That's the last man who's ever goin' to lay a hand on me without me invitin' him first."

"Miss Pepper, maybe you ought to go back to Denver. I hear they got all sorts of respectable jobs in Denver these days."

"No cities. No saloons. No crowded rooms. I want the wide open skies and a warm fireplace. This is big country. . . . There's got to be room for everyone out here. Even someone like me."

"You know, I heard a man say that up in Wyomin' there's some women homesteadin' their own place. Maybe you could go up there. Say, you got any money, Miss Pepper? I got five cash dollars, and you know you're welcome to it."

Pepper gazed back at Suzanne Cedar's leather valise.

"No, Stack, thank you. I have some money. Now what did you tell me about this McCurley fellow's place?"

"I hear he opened a nice little hotel and eatin' place over by the North Platte. It ain't no dive."

"Could you drive me over there?"

"Surely. You want that job after all?"

"No, I want to rent a buggy. Do you think

he'll have any horses?"

"I reckon so, Miss Pepper. You fixin' to go for a ride?"

"Yeah. I've got a ranch I've just got to take a look at. Stack, I've got to ask you to do me a big favor. Can you help me?"

"Yes, ma'am . . . I'll help if I can. What do you want me to do for you?"

"Lie."

"Come again?"

"I need you to tell this Bob McCurley fellow that my name is Suzanne Cedar and I just came in from Denver. Please, Stack, can you do that?"

He was silent for a couple minutes.

"Sure, Miss Pepper, I'll tell him. Shoot, how do I know what your real name is?"

"It's Aimee. Aimee Paige."

"That's a pretty name. It sounds like one of them San Francisco society ladies. You don't think my mama named me Stack, do ya? My real name's Henry."

"How did you get the name Stack?"

"I was bouncing drunks in Seattle. You ever been there? Don't go there, Miss Pepper. It's a mean town. Well, every night I'd haul out five or six and just stack them up like cordwood on the wharf. So they started calling me Stack. How about you; how did you get to be Pepper?"

"I don't remember too much. On my first day in school, when I was just a little girl, this big kid grabbed my pigtails and teased me about my yellow hair."

"So what did you do?"

"I busted his nose 'til it bled, and he ran home crying. From then on, everybody just seemed intent on calling me Pepper."

"So now you're going to be Miss Suzanne Cedar and find a rancher husband? Danni Mae told me a little about that gal we buried."

"I'm going to give it a try, Stack. I could make a man a good wife. I can cook. I can sew. I can ride. I can work hard. And you know I can dance."

"Miss Pepper, you can dance like no other girl can dance."

She took a deep breath and sighed.

"Am I just kiddin' myself, Stack? Do you really think I could pull it off?"

"Yep. Providin' that he don't pull your pigtails and make fun of yer yeller hair." He grinned.

It was almost dark when they rolled into Bob McCurley's place. It was the proprietor himself who met them at the stable.

"Well, Stack Lowery! I never thought I'd see you this far west."

"Oh, the pass got washed out, and we need some supplies, Mr. McCurley."

"You'll be spending the night then?"

"I'll just bunk in the barn, if you don't mind. But this lady will need a room for the night."

"Surely." McCurley tipped his hat to Pepper and stared at her. "Eh . . . it seems like I should know your name, ma'am. Have we met? I'm Bob McCurley."

Sitting straight-backed and tipping her head only slightly, she smiled. "I'm Miss Suzanne Cedar. I'm afraid I'm so new around here I don't know a soul."

"I knowed it! I knowed it! Why, I almost guessed you was the one!"

"The one what?"

"The one with golden hair and green eyes. Early this morning a fella came in for supplies. He just bought a ranch north of here, and he said he was lookin' out for a green-eyed, golden-haired lady by the name of Suzanne Cedar. And, ma'am, you're jist as pretty as he described. Let's see, what was his name? Hancock? No . . . Hatcher! That's it. Zachariah Hatcher!"

"He was here?"

"Yes, miss, and I do declare he was anxious to see you."

"Is it possible to ride out to that ranch this evening?"

"Eh . . . no, miss, I'm afraid it would take the most part of a day. Now I'm not real sure where the place is, but from the description, it would be just about on the state line."

"Well, in that case," Pepper responded, "I'd like to have a room for the night."

That evening at the supper table Pepper was introduced to the other guests as Miss Suzanne Cedar. The meal was tasty, the conversation light and pleasant, the company congenial.

Later, in her well-furnished large room, she lay under clean cotton sheets amidst ruffles and lace and stared at the dark ceiling. Everything seemed so peaceful.

No shots fired in the street.

No fights downstairs.

No women screaming, cussing, or crying.

And none of the men tried to waltz her up to her bedroom.

Miss Cedar, I enjoyed being you tonight. Those people thought I was somebody important. The men were polite, the women, courteous. No one was drunk. I fancied their words, and they seemed to appreciate mine. Now by tomorrow night, this game might be over, but at least I got to have one night at bein' somethin' other than a dance-hall girl.

I like it.

I like it very much.

From her second-story window facing the mountains, Pepper saw Stack Lowery leave right after daylight. She waved, but he didn't see her. She opened her window slightly, allowing the chilled air to cool her. Pinning her hair behind her head and wearing the only dress she owned that was too modest for the dance-hall crowd, she went downstairs to breakfast.

"Will you be goin' out to Hatcher's ranch today, miss?" Bob McCurley asked.

"I know this must all sound strange, but Mr. Hatcher and I just keep missing connections, so I will need to ride out there."

"If you like, the wife and I could drive you in the buggy. We ain't been in this country too long ourselves, and we've been meanin' to see that district up on the state line."

"Oh . . . Mr. McCurley . . . that's mighty generous of you. I just couldn't ask you to do that!"

"You ain't askin'," McCurley insisted. "I'm offerin'. That's an entirely different matter."

"Well . . . if you put it that way, I'd be as happy as a . . . I'd be delighted."

By 9:30 A.M. Pepper was riding comfortably on the back bench of a two-seat carriage with Mr. and Mrs. McCurley sitting up front. By the time they stopped to rest the horses and have a nooner, she had told them the entire story of the correspondence with Zachariah Hatcher and the decision to get married.

"Well," Bob McCurley responded, "ranchers can get to be a real crusty lot. Hope you got a strong back and plenty of sand."

"It sounds terribly romantic to me, Miss Cedar," Mrs. McCurley interjected. "None of us really know each other too well before we get married, no matter how many times we've been together. When will the wedding be?"

"I ain't rightly . . . eh . . . ," Pepper stammered. "We will have to make that decision after we've had time to talk. I'm really gettin', eh . . . getting a little nervous."

I should never have had them come out here! If Hatcher doesn't buy this Suzanne Cedar impression, I'll — I'll curl up and die! It's got to work! It's just got to!

"Looks like a rider comin' in from the north." Bob McCurley pointed with his knife blade, which served as his eating utensil.

"Two of them, isn't there, Robert?" Mrs. McCurley questioned.

"Nope, jist one. Leadin' a horse. It looks like . . . Hey, that's him! That's Hatcher. That's Onespot. Sold him that horse yesterday!"

Pepper's pulse quickened "Are you sure?" She could feel tufts of short blonde hair that never would stay in place on the back of her neck begin to tingle.

"Yep. That there is Zachariah Hatcher, all right. Came out lookin' fer ya, he did."

"Oh, my, this is frightfully exciting!" Mrs.

McCurley squealed. "Who knows what will happen?"

You're right about that, darlin'. This has the potential of being the worst day of an already lousy life!

"You ladies stay here. I'll walk out there and welcome him in."

I should have put on that strong perfume! I knew I should have. Why didn't I remember?

"Mrs. McCurley, should I take off my hat? Is my hair straight? Should I sit down? How do I look?"

"Like a nervous bride, of course. Just stand right there and let him come to you."

"Hatcher?"

"McCurley. I didn't expect to find a picnic this far north." Tap nodded, staring at the two women in the distance.

"Ain't no picnic, son. We are headin' toward your place with a friend of yours!" McCurley beamed.

My word . . . it is her! It's Miss Suzanne Cedar herself. She's even more beautiful than I imagined! All right, Tapadera Andrews . . . the next two minutes may decide the next twenty years. Slow and easy. What would Zachariah Hatcher do in this situation?

Pepper stood next to Mrs. McCurley, nervously twisting Suzanne Cedar's engagement ring on her finger.

Relax, girl. Take deep breaths. You can do it. You've been pretending every night for years. This is the big one. He's strong — look at those shoulders! And handsome. My goodness, she done herself real proud by him. What would Miss Suzanne Cedar do now? Does she curtsy? Shake his hand? Throw her arms around him? Would she kiss him? Will he really think I'm Suzanne?

The two men walked slowly to the women.

"Eh, humph." McCurley cleared his throat. "I knowed you two ain't ever met, so let me make it official. Mr. Zachariah Hatcher, let me present to you Miss Suzanne Cedar. Miss Cedar, this is Mr. Hatcher."

Tap Andrews stared into the green eyes of Aimee "Pepper" Paige.

She's tired. She's worried. Maybe she knows! Maybe she's trying to figure me out. Maybe she's disappointed in what she sees. My goodness, my goodness, she is a beautiful lady. It's got to work. It's just got to.

Pepper wanted to say something, but no words came to mind.

His eyes are older than the rest of him. He's spent lots of time out in the open. He's troubled. I disappoint him. He was expecting someone else. Here it comes. I wish I was

89

back at April's. I wish all I had to worry about was the likes of Jordan Beckett and Selena Oatley. Please like me; please say something . . . I'm going to die!

"Well, are you two jist goin' to stand there gawkin?" McCurley prodded.

"Eh . . . Miss Cedar . . . I'm just so nervous I don't know what to say. I, eh . . . I'm just taken back by how downright pretty you are. It's kind of like I never thought this day would ever come."

He thinks I'm her! He really does. I can see it in his eyes.

A wide smile broke over Pepper's face as she began to relax.

"Mr. Hatcher . . . my heart is pounding still. I've been thinking and dreaming about this moment for a long, long time. Now that it's here . . . I'm so happy! I think I'm going to faint!"

"Well, if you two don't hug or somethin', we'll all faint," Mrs. McCurley insisted. "Me and Robert will tend the horses."

Tap walked over to Pepper. She held out both hands, and he took them into his own. For another moment they just stared.

What would Hatcher do?

Is he going to stand there all day? Suzanne, oh, Suzanne, what would you do if you were me?

"Suzanne?"

90

"Yes, Zach?"

"I don't know the procedure. Would it be proper for me to give you a hug?"

"I believe so."

Tap pulled her close and put his arms around her shoulders. She slipped her arms around his waist, and they held each other tight. He thought he heard some songbirds singing nearby, but then decided it was just the ringing noise in his ears.

4

After several awkward attempts at conversations, the four were on the trail to the ranch. Tap and Pepper rode the horses about fifty feet ahead of the buggy occupied by Robert and Mrs. McCurley.

"What's the ranch like?"

"I'm sorry about your father."

"Is it as pretty a country as this?"

"Ah . . . your mother's doin' all right in Chicago, is she?"

"Did you get any cows yet?"

"I hope you had a nice train ride out. I've never been on the train too much."

"What about those bulls down in Arizona?"

"I'm sorry but I never . . . eh, you know . . . ran across your brother, eh, Abel."

"Did you ever try to sleep on a train?"

"I hope you didn't get stuck in the rough part of Denver."

"Is the ranch very far from here?"

"Fort Collins is a little nicer, but personally I'd just as soon stay away from both of them. Yep, give me the wide open country any day."

"Do we have any neighbors?"

"I'm sorry I didn't get to Fort Collins in time. There was this Indian trouble down in Arizona."

"Is the house nice? I hope the roof doesn't leak. I have nightmares about roofs leaking."

"We had to shoot our way out of the desert."

"How far to the nearest town? We don't have to go to Denver, do we? I don't like Denver."

"I tried to clean the place up a bit, but I'm not used to having to keep things lady-clean."

"I don't guess I'll ever see my brother . . . eh, Abel, again. Something must have happened to him."

"A couple of hands from the Rafter R Ranch came over for a visit, but that's quite a distance."

"Did you buy this horse just for me?"

"You ought to see the sunsets at the ranch . . . Oh, I guess there's plenty of time for that."

"Well, he's not like the horses in Tennessee . . . I mean Kentucky . . . eh, I sold them to some folks in Tennessee."

"Sure seems strange for the two of us to be ridin' up this trail together, doesn't it?"

"What's his name?"

"I want you to make a list of what we

need to buy for the ranch house. It looks to me like it's been a while since a woman was there. How did you get to McCurley's anyway? Are they running a stage that far?"

"You'll have to tell me about California. I ain't . . . I mean, I . . . haven't ever been there. Well, I mean, of course, I've never been anywhere but back East."

"Onespot."

"I took a stage, but there was a wreck. I don't think I want to go on that road again. I talk too much when I'm nervous . . . oh, heavens . . . am I nervous!"

"We sure do have got a lot to talk about."

"Do you think this is a good idea? I mean . . . we don't know each other very well, do we, Mr. Hatcher?"

"Well, Miss Cedar, at this rate were goin' to know ever'thing about each other in about twenty minutes." Andrews grinned and took a big, deep breath.

Suddenly neither of them said a word. They rode silently for several minutes.

Well, Pepper, old girl, that went pretty well. I don't think he suspects anything. I wonder what he looks like with a shave? At least I ain't stuck with no rotten-toothed potbelly. I sure do hope he don't have a mean streak. Boise City Stella ran off with that mean lawyer, and we never heard from her again. I hope he doesn't hurt me none.

The black horse had a smooth gait, and

Pepper enjoyed the bouncing rhythm. The countryside was more open than around Pingree Hill, but she had spent most of her time indoors. The fresh air seemed to help her breathe easily and see more clearly. Sometimes during the conversation it was almost as if she were at a distance watching the two of them ride along.

He's a fine-lookin' man, really. In a drover sort of way. I mean, I can't imagine him in a suit and tie, except at the weddin', of course.

Tap glanced over at the McCurley's buggy. Then he turned back in the saddle.

Zachariah Hatcher . . . what do you know about that? I think I pulled it off. She's riding right along with the whole thing. Yes, sir, I think it can work. Now if we can just get settled into the ranch without many visits or interruptions, maybe . . . she's a looker, all right. I wonder what that yellow hair looks like tousled down on her shoulders? I can't believe she'd come out west searchin' for a husband! Why, I've seen popular dance-hall girls that weren't half that pretty. I surely hope she don't have a wanderin' eye. Some women that good lookin' just naturally . . . but not her. Miss Cedar is a God-fearin' lady. Kind of like an angel in disguise. Yes, sir, this is too good to be true.

Tap tried to remember the last time he

was out pleasure riding with such a quality woman. His review of ladies seldom brought back more than dance-hall memories.

There are days when the world seems to be going your way, your horse has a skip of celebration, the wind tastes as sweet as icing on a cake, and all the sights you lay your eyes on hang prominently in your memory forever.

This was one of those days. Tap tried to keep from constantly gaping at her.

Women don't like men to stare at them — makes 'em nervous. But I reckon Miss Suzanne Cedar has spent most of her life with men gawkin' at her. Pretty face, pretty figure. No wonder old Hatcher was hesitant about his shortcut to Heaven.

"Eh, Mr. Hatcher . . . I was wonderin' . . . without bein' too presumin' . . . are we going to have a real church wedding? I mean, if you like me . . . you know . . . if we decide . . . like you said in your letters . . . you know, to go ahead with it?"

Church? Oh, man . . . church? I don't even know where the nearest one is!

"You know, Miss Cedar . . . eh, Suzanne . . . that, ah . . . brings up something that's been eatin' on me."

"What's that, Mr. Hatcher?"

"There's one thing I didn't put in the

96

letters that I should have. You're bound to find out sooner or later, and I wanted you to hear it from me first."

"You robbed a bank?" she gasped.

"Oh, no, that's not, eh . . . exactly it. It's just that I sort of got a name, well, like a nickname, that ever'one who knows me calls me, and I was a little embarrassed to tell you straight up."

"A nickname?"

"Yeah, Miss Cedar, everyone just calls me Tap."

"What?"

"Tap. You know, like in tapadera? These leather stirrup covers are called tapaderas. But a horsewoman like you knew that . . . Anyway, if it's agreeable to you, I'd rather be called Tap than Zachariah."

She put her hand over her mouth to keep from giggling, but she couldn't hold it in. Finally she burst out in laughter.

"I know it kind of seems funny, and if you'd rather not, I could —"

"No, no, no," she said chuckling. "That's not it . . . wait . . . really, Tap. I like that name. I really do. It fits you. Listen." She took a deep breath. "I was laughing because I was afraid to tell you something, too."

"Well, did you rob a bank?" he teased.

"No, it's the nickname thing," she confessed with a smile.

"You mean you have a nickname, too?"

"Yeah, and you probably won't be able to guess what it is."

"Eh . . . you sort of look like a princess, but more, more . . . well, even better. I know what it is — Angel!"

"What did you call me?" Her smile fell flat.

"I was just guessing that they called you Angel. I didn't mean any disrespect."

Then she flashed a wide smile. "No, no, it's all right. You just caught me by surprise. My nickname is Pepper."

"Pepper? Like in black pepper? Chili pepper?"

"Yeah, but if you don't like it, we can —"

"Don't like it? It's nickel-plated. You're a little too refined for a name like that, of course, so it gives you a hint of mystery. I like that."

"A hint of mystery? Mr. Hatcher . . . I mean, Tap . . . you aren't trying to sweet-talk me, are you?"

"Of course, I am." He grinned. "Isn't that what I'm supposed to do . . . Pepper?"

"Yeah, it's kind of fun, ain't . . . I mean, isn't it?"

The conversation back to the ranch was nonstop from both sides — dealing with everything from the best breed of cattle for the northern ranges to the best color for kitchen curtains. There was a lot of talking, not much listening, and plenty of sideward glances for quick inspections.

They finally came to the base of the canyon that led up to the ranch. Tap reined his brown horse and waited for the carriage to catch up.

"Sorry, folks, I didn't mean to ignore you. We were just tryin' to get caught up knowin' each other." He grinned.

"No problem, Hatcher." Bob McCurley winked. "Say, do you go by Zach?"

"Actually, as I was telling Miss Cedar, most folks call me Tap. It's sort of a nickname. And come to find out, she's called Pepper. Isn't that a great name?"

"Tap and Pepper — yes, that sounds very nice indeed." Mrs. McCurley nodded. "You two must have been planning the wedding."

"Oh — wedding! Yes," Pepper added. "We got sidetracked. Tap, where is the closest church?"

"Church?" Bob McCurley coughed. "There ain't no church for a hundred miles at least!"

"Eh . . . I'm afraid Bob's right," Tap agreed.

"But we do get a travelin' preacher now and then," Mrs. McCurley hurried to explain. "I'm sure the Reverend would do the honors."

"I figured we might just get the parson to do the service out at the ranch . . . providin' that's acceptable to you. Now I know you're used to more than that back home, but it's kind of all we have."

"Oh, well . . . yes, I can see the necessity, but —"

"You're disappointed, aren't you?" Tap asked.

"No, no, it's not that. I was wondering how we can make plans, not knowing when the Reverend might come by."

"Don't you worry about it, honey," Mrs. McCurley replied. "The good Lord will help you work it out. Isn't that right, Robert?"

"Yep. I reckon you're right about that."

Tap pushed back his wide-brimmed gray hat and wiped his brow. "Listen, I've sort of neglected my duties here. You are all plannin' to spend the night at the ranch, aren't ya? I mean, I wouldn't want you drivin' down this road after dark. It isn't much more than a wagon rut from here on up to the place."

"Thank you, yes, we will stay," Mrs. McCurley accepted. "Listen, I don't want to be presumptive, but maybe Miss, I mean, perhaps Pepper would like to ride in the carriage for a while. I don't know about her, but some of us ladies can only take so many hours on a horse."

"Oh . . . yes, of course! Pepper, I'm surely sorry. As you can see, I'm not exactly used to ridin' with a lady like yourself," Tap apologized.

"Well . . ." *Oh, thank you, thank you, thank you! Mrs. McCurley, you deserve a prize!* "Perhaps I should try to be a little more hospitable to the McCurleys."

Tap tied Onespot to the back of the buggy and helped Pepper get situated.

"Maybe I ought to just ride up there and get a fire started in the cookstove. I didn't know for sure I'd have company today. You folks got to realize I just bought the place, and it's not as deluxe as the McCurley Hotel."

"Hatcher, there ain't no need to apologize," Bob McCurley assured him. "Now go get the coffee boilin'. We'll be along right away."

"You'll be able to see the ranch from the top of that ridge." Tap pointed to a rise in the trail. "But you'll still have about three more miles to go."

He stared at Pepper for a moment.

"Why, Mr. Hatcher, I do believe you're gawking at me."

"Pepper, you're just about the prettiest Baptist lady I ever met."

Good heavens, am I a Baptist? I don't remember that in the letters!

Tap turned his brown horse north and spurred to a fast trot. He sat up straight and tall in the saddle.

This must be the way it feels when you discover gold . . . or when you win that big pot at poker after gamblin' your last dollar — sort of like having all your dreams come true. Tap, old boy, that Indian ambush in Arizona might end up being the best thing that ever happened to you!

Let's see, it's too late to soak beans . . . I guess I'll just let the ladies cook what they want.

Cresting the trail, Tap parked his pony as he surveyed the distant ranch. The wide valley before him stretched all the way to Wyoming. The Medicine Bow Mountains on the east showed plenty of timber. The mountains on the left weren't as tall — had only a scattering of juniper, scrub cedar, and piñon pines. Most of the crest showed great granite outcroppings.

It's a ranch with clear geographic borders, plenty of water, and . . . What? Horses! Horses in the corral? Have I got company? I was just here. What are they doin' in my barn? Maybe it's their ranch! They don't look like hands. Not now! Not with Pepper here. I've got to send them on their way before Pepper and the McCurleys pull in!

He spun the horse around and galloped back to the others.

"What's the matter?" McCurley asked.

"Look, there are some men at the ranch.

They moved in to the corral with a dozen horses. I need to ride up and find out what's going on. From a distance they look like drifters. Bob, you keep the ladies up there on the promontory. Don't come in until it looks clear."

"What do we do if something happens to you?" McCurley asked.

"Then take this wagon and run for it. Bob, you'll have to protect the women."

"How do you know these men are violent?" Mrs. McCurley quizzed.

"I don't . . . but I've seen a lot of men on the prowl. Anyway, I don't want to take any chance with your safety."

"I've heard rumors of a rough bunch robbin' banks up on the border. But I don't think they'd be down here. You sure you don't want me to come, Tap?" McCurley asked again.

"Nope. This is one I've got to settle on my own," he answered.

He rode back up to the top of the ridge. As he did, he pulled his rifle from the scabbard and laid it across his lap.

It wasn't the first time he ever rode single-handed against a gang. There were the Stocktons down at Santa Fe, the Babbs and Donovan gang over in Virginia City . . . even Kansas Dick and that bunch.

Only one or two have the drive to shoot face to face. The others will hesitate. But I've

103

got to find those one or two!

As he approached, Tap counted six horses in the corral and five saddled and tied out front. Only three men stood outside the barn.

He rode straight to the house and dismounted, keeping the horse between himself and the others, tied Brownie to the post, and then walked right at the men, still carrying his Winchester on his right shoulder.

"Git right back on that pony and ride, mister!"

Tap kept walking toward them. He'd spent his whole life looking into the dirty stubbled beards and narrow eyes of men like these.

"Mister," one of the men called out when he was still seventy feet from the barn, "you made one big mistake ridin' in here. And if you even think of pointin' that rifle at one of us, it will be the last mistake you ever make!"

Without a moment's hesitation Tap pulled the hammer back on the already-cocked rifle. Immediately, all three men grabbed for their revolvers.

"The first gun that comes out of the holster, that fat man with tobacco stains on his vest gets a .44-40 in the gut . . . you understand that? And I'm talkin' to those in the barn, too. You two get out here where

I can see ya! Now what are you doin' on my ranch?"

"Your ranch?" The nervous fat man at the barn door faked a smile. "Ain't nobody at this place since old Tucker left the country."

"You're wrong. It's mine now. And I want to know what you're doin' here."

"Well," the one at the far left spoke as he sidestepped to cut wide behind Andrews, "we're jist going to use the corral to hold our spare ponies for a few days. We'll come back and pick them up — don't you worry none."

"You take one more step to circle me, and you'll never live to eat supper! Do you understand that? Now whether you boys are smart enough to rob a bank or a stage, I'm not sure, but you aren't using this corral for relay horses."

The last thing on earth I need is some posse ridin' in here.

"Just chalk it up to experience," Andrews continued, "and head down the trail. From now on, this part of the county is off-limits. It's that simple. I'll give you ten minutes to ride over that hill."

"Mister," the fat man sneered, "you obviously don't know who you're dealin' with. We ride with Jordan Beckett. Does that mean anything to you?"

Suddenly Andrews spun to the right and fired the Winchester at the corral of horses. The rifle went to his left hand, and with his right he pulled his Colt and had it pointed at the fat man before any of the stunned men got their own guns out of the holster.

"You shot one of our horses!" the fat man screamed.

"You got nine minutes left."

"You're a fool! Five to one odds you can't . . ." As the fat man began to speak, Andrews walked straight up to him. The man started to pull his gun, but the barrel of Andrews's Winchester caught the man in the wrist. There was a sickening crack and a cry of pain.

At that moment, Tap saw a thin man with a wispy blond mustache to the right pulling his gun. Andrews dove to the ground, and the bullet buzzed over him, tearing into the leg of one of the others who had been attempting to circle him.

"You shot me! You crazy Texan, you —"

Andrews came to his feet behind the fat man and jammed the barrel of the Colt behind the man's right ear.

"Get 'em out of here, fat man. Get 'em out of here right now, or there'll be more than horses that die!" .

"You're crazy," the man hollered, still clutching his broken wrist. "You're a dead man, mister!"

"Help me, Payton. I'm bleedin' to death!" cried the man who was shot.

"Let me tell you what's crazy — you boys

106

got most all of northern Colorado to hide that relay of horses. I don't give a cow chip how many banks or trains or stages you rob. I just said you can't cache horses on my place. It isn't worth gettin' shot up over, and it isn't worth losin' another horse! I want to see you movin' now!"

The tallest man, still back in the shadow of the barn, started to pull his revolver, but Andrews's bullet ripped through the man's arm, and he staggered back and fell to the dirt.

"Look, that could just as easily have been in the forehead, but I got company comin' and don't want to have to dig a grave."

Years of facing down gunmen had taught Tap to sense the exact moment when the battle was over. He could tell by their eyes that the fighting was done.

"Now, I'm not — oh, now look at that!" Andrews pointed to the distant ridge where the McCurley buggy and spare horse could be seen.

The gunmen glanced up at the silhouette.

"Company's startin' to come in, and I don't even have the coffee boilin'. I just don't have time for this, boys. I'm going to have to kill you all and bury you in the mornin'."

"Wait!" the fat man cried out. "We're leavin'."

"I can't ride! I been shot in the leg. Payton, you got to help me!"

"He's right — he can't ride," Andrews insisted. "Just leave him, Payton. I'll take care of him. I'll bury him out by that little clump of pines."

"Payton! Help me up. Don't leave me with this crazy man!"

Within sixty seconds all five, including the two wounded men, were mounted and the extra horses turned out.

"You ride east, over that draw in the distance . . . and don't waste a second thought about coming back," Andrews ordered holding the rifle to his shoulder.

"Oh, we'll be back, mister, and you'll wish your mama never gave you birth."

The explosion from Andrews's rifle dropped a swayed-back blue roan from the remuda of horses. The other four bolted to the east ahead of the riders.

"You killed another horse!" the fat man shouted.

Andrews could feel the back of his neck flush with anger. "Don't you ever, ever bring my mama, rest her soul, into the conversation!"

"We'll be back —"

"Boys, I already figure you for not bein' the smartest in the world. But that's tolerable because this country has many a man who isn't too bright. But if any of you ever come on this ranch again, you will prove beyond all shadow of doubt that you are the stupidest men in the world. You boys have seen these peep sights, haven't ya? It means I can bring you down at a thousand yards. Now you remember that next time you get within 999 yards of this place!"

"Jordan Beckett will hear about this," the man growled as he turned to ride off.

Tell him the Triple Creek Ranch is off-limits and that he really ought to hire some men with a few brains. Now just in case you were wonderin', fat man, my peep sight will be aimed at the back of your head all the way up that incline. And at any point if I happen to get a little restless, you'll be facing the judgment seat before the sun goes down."

A black-vested man turned his horse around and growled, "I ain't goin' to take any more of this." And he started to pull his gun.

"Texas, don't!" the fat man screamed. "We cain't lose any more horses!" Texas removed his hand from his gun.

Tap watched through the peep sight of the rifle as the men rode up the hill and disappeared. Finally, he lowered his gun, folded back the tang sight, and walked back toward the house. Pushing his hat to the back of his head, he looked up at the wagon still a mile from the ranch buildings.

Tap! I'm not sure you looked like a God-

109

fearin' Zachariah Hatcher. You can't go through life wantin' to shoot every man who comes against you. You've got to do better than that. If you're going to try to be Hatcher, you've got to think like him, act like him, talk like him. Slow it down, Tap. Keep out of trouble.

Leading Brownie to the barn, he pulled off the saddle and turned the horse out into the corral. He tossed his saddlebag over his shoulder, picked up the Winchester, and walked back to the house, stopping in front of the barn to pick up three brass .44 casings and shove them into his pocket.

"Hatcher!" Bob McCurley called as they drove into the yard. "Are you all right?"

Tap noticed that McCurley had a shotgun across his lap now. "Yep. Just a little misunderstandin', that's all."

"Misunderstanding?" Pepper gasped.

"The way I seen it, you shot two of them and two horses and chased the whole bunch out," McCurley reported.

"Well . . . one of 'em shot another one in the leg, but the rest of the story stands."

"My heavens," Mrs. McCurley exclaimed, "who were they?"

"The best that I could figure it, they were some gang of outlaws who have been usin' this place for a relay of horses. I told them to leave —"

"Relay horses?" Pepper interrupted. "I don't understand."

"Well, a gang will rob a bank or a stage or a train and then hit the trail to escape. Naturally, a posse will set out after them, but the robbers stash a relay team or two of horses along their trail so they can always have fresh mounts. That way no posse will ever catch them."

Pepper tilted her head and quizzed, "How do you know so much about this sort of thing?"

"Oh, w-well," Tap stammered, "it happens all the time."

"It happens all the time? You mean, men ridin' into your ranch and you havin' a shootout happens often?"

"No, no, miss . . . no," Tap tried to clarify. "It happens fairly often in other places where I've been. I didn't know there was anything close enough worth stealin' around here. I wouldnt think it was very common here. . . eh, is it McCurley?"

"We ain't never had a bit of trouble down our way, no, miss," the hotel owner advised. "And don't you worry none, Miss Pepper. This here Hatcher just handled himself about as slick with a gun as any man I've seen, and believe me, I've seen some good ones."

Oh, brother, I blew it now. There's no way some timid lady from the East will want to live in this place. What would Hatcher do now?

"Well, to tell you the truth, I kind of surprised myself," Tap began. "I'm not always so quick-tempered, but after all this time of waitin' for Miss Cedar, and what with finally getting the ranch . . . I guess it drove me to be a little aggressive in protectin' things. The good Lord must have been watchin' over me."

I surely hope that convinces her!

"It answered any question I had about what we do when trouble comes," Pepper said with a nod. "Will they be comin' back?"

"I don't think so. There's no gain for them. They'll just stake those ponies in another canyon or draw. Now, Bob, if you'll turn your team out and pull down some hay, I'll start that coffee boilin' and give the ladies a tour of the house."

Tap helped Mrs. McCurley down from the buggy. He noticed that her hands were tough and callused like the hard land she had lived in for years. Then he turned to Pepper and assisted her to the ground.

Tough and tender. Soft, yet strong. She hasn't worked with those Kentucky horses too much, yet I bet she could drag you around by the ear without straining.

"Ladies, this won't take long," he announced. "This is the front porch, which just happens to afford a nice view of the settin' sun if you perch down there at the far end." Tap swung open the door to the big front room. "Now this is the living room, parlor, dining room, and just about any-thing-else-you-want-to-do-in-it room."

"Oh, my, it's so huge, Mr. Hatcher," Mrs. McCurley exclaimed. "Why, you could open a stage stop with a room like this! And the fireplace! The rock work is very well done. What do you think, Pepper?"

What do I think? I've worked in dance halls smaller than this. It's wonderful!
"Eh . . . it's very nice. Could use a little more furniture, I believe," she com-mented.

"You're right about that, Pepper. Maybe you and Mrs. McCurley could make a list of items needed. Some of 'em I can make, and others we'll try to buy."

Then he led them to the right hand door at the back of the living room. "Now this is . . . well, obviously it's the bedroom. I'll have to apologize to you and Bob that I don't have a guest room to offer you. At least not yet."

"Well, now this is good-sized, too!" Mrs. McCurley gushed.

"And what a long built-in dresser," Pep-per noted.

"Now don't you mind, Tap," Mrs. McCur-ley continued. "I'm sure us ladies can get along in here just fine tonight. You men will have to make pallets in the living room or sleep out in the barn."

We will? Oh . . . until the wedding . . . it's certainly what Hatcher would do. This is gettin' tougher than I thought.

"Yes, ma'am, you ladies just make yourself at home. Let me show you the kitchen." Tap led them back out into the main room and around into the kitchen.

As they walked into the room, the big gray and white cat leaped from the counter and sped out the back door.

Ignoring the cat, Pepper commented, "My, there are lots of cupboards!"

A cat? He has a cat? Am I supposed to know its name? I'll just wait until I hear Tap call it by name.

"Well, there seems to be plenty of dishes, but they aren't many of them alike, so maybe you ladies can tell me what's missin' there, too. The supplies are in that back cupboard. I'll stoke this wood stove, and maybe I could impose on you to stir up some supper."

Andrews and McCurley sat by a fire in the main room sipping coffee while the women busied themselves in the kitchen. McCurley motioned to Tap, and both men stepped out to the front porch carrying their coffee.

"You got a nice spread here, Hatcher."

"Thanks, Bob. There's a lot of work to do, but I've got a lifetime to do it in."

"I surely hope so."

"What do you mean?"

McCurley leaned up against a porch post and took another sip of his Arbuckles. "Well, sir, I weren't exactly truthful back there with the ladies about them outlaws."

"How's that?"

"If it's the same bunch I've been hearing about, they're bad, real bad. They're the type that will shoot ya just for the fun of it. Since they've been runnin' the border, all sorts of folks have showed up dead."

"Why do they come clear out here? There isn't nothin' worth stealin', is there?"

"Nope. But there ain't no lawman for a hundred miles in any direction. And no one in the district will face them down. So they ride off and do their stealin' up in Wyoming, Montana, Idaho, or Utah and then come high-tailing it back in here to hole up."

"Where's their camp?"

"Don't rightly know that . . . but they seem to hang out over at Pingree Hill."

"Where's that?" Tap asked.

"About seventy, eighty miles east of here . . . There's a dance hall, a regular hurdy-gurdy house, and a few other buildings. It's a rough bunch that holes up there. They been havin' so much trouble with the stage that they're thinkin' of canceling the run."

Tap tipped his tin cup and gulped down the last dregs of his now-cold coffee, filtering the grounds with his teeth. "You ever heard of a Jordan Beckett?"

"He's the worst of the lot, so I'm told. Never met the man and don't hope to. Where'd you come by his name?"

"Those five that I chased off claimed to be working for Beckett."

"He's a mean one. Rumor is they robbed a mine payroll up near Helena, and Beckett shot and killed the bookkeeper after he was roped and tied. There's something missing in a man who would do that. You can bet he'll be back out to visit you."

"That's kind of what I'm expectin'." Tap walked out toward the hitching post as McCurley followed. "Bob, have you got a room that Pepper could rent for a few weeks — until we get this weddin' all planned and completed? I figure it would be good to keep her away from the ranch as much as possible until I see which way the wind blows with this gang."

"We're way ahead of you. We got the room already reserved. We knowed you two wouldn't want to do nothin' to cast dispersion on Miss Cedar's virtue."

"Eh . . . right . . . that's what I meant," Tap sputtered.

"Now let me tell you somethin' else I didn't tell the ladies," McCurley continued. He leaned so close to Andrews that he could smell the coffee from the old mans' breath. "That weren't the first gunfight you ever faced."

"Nope. I've had my share, but it's all in the past now. I'd prefer not to worry Miss Pepper too much."

"Well, I catch your drift there. But I don't know if even you can face them down again by yourself."

"Bob, if some two-bit gang can chase me off my property, well, I want to find out as soon as possible. If I can't keep this place safe, I have no right to bring a lady on it."

"Be mighty careful, son. That ain't no two-bit gang. Next time they won't stand out in the open and let you take shots at 'em. No, sir, every one of 'em will shoot you in the back if they can!" Then McCurley looked over at the barn. "You got a couple of horses to bury."

"Yep . . . but I figure they'll wait 'til mornin." Both men turned back to the front of the house. "Thanks for not puttin' any more fear into Pepper. I'm frettin' that she will want to go back east. She's a little timid about all this, you know."

"Could of fooled me." McCurley grinned.

117

"She comes across as a determined lady. You watch — she'll make it."

"You two out surveying the landscape? Come in here and wash up. It's supper time," Mrs. McCurley commanded.

The lamps were lit before they finished eating. Tap was amazed that the women could scrape together such a fine meal out of his meager supplies. There was meat, boiled potatoes and carrots, pan bread, and canned tomatoes with some kind of seasoning he couldn't identify. The big gray and white cat sat most of the time near his side, but no one ever mentioned it.

"We'll be needin' to get back on the road right after daylight in the mornin'," Bob McCurley announced. "We've got a business to run, and the hired help seems to always have something bust when we're gone."

"I hear you made some arrangements to stay at the McCurleys' hotel until the parson rides through," Tap said to Pepper.

I did? Why would I want . . . oh, yeah.

"Oh, I hope we weren't presumptive," Mrs. McCurley added. "I assumed that . . ."

"Oh, my, yes . . . you certainly assumed correctly, Mrs. McCurley. I was so anxious to get out here yesterday I forgot to make proper arrangements."

"Will you be sending for your other things?"

"My other things?"

"Your trunks, clothing, personal items, and the like?"

"Oh . . . my . . . I keep forgetting. So much else on my mind. Yes, of course, they're at the Wemberly House in Fort Collins. I do hope I can send for them without going back. The road is terrible. I never want to go down there again! Did I tell you the stage had a terrible wreck?"

"I believe you did," Tap replied.

"And then we had to stop for a while at that horrid roadhouse at Pingree Hill. I, for one, will never step into a place like that again," Pepper insisted.

"Robert told me it's a regular hurdy-gurdy over there," Tap offered.

"Did he mention how he knew so much about it?" Mrs. McCurley demanded.

Bob McCurley sat straight up in his chair and looked at his wife. "Why, I've heard others talk. That's how! You know me better than that, Mrs. McCurley."

"Well, I hear that might be the hangout of those boys who rode in here," Tap added.

"No! Are you sure?" Pepper gasped.

"They mentioned they were workin' for an hombre named Jordan Beckett, and Bob said he's a regular over there."

Jordan Beckett! Oh . . . no! No . . . no, no!

*He'll ruin it all! He'll come over and shoot
. . . I don't want him ever to enter my life
again.*

Pepper's stomach twisted into knots, and
her head began to pound. She took several
deep breaths.

"Are you all right, Miss Pepper? You look
pallid."

"Well, the poor dear has gone through
quite a tough week. Honey, you go on and
lie down for a while. I'll straighten up here,"
Mrs. McCurley suggested.

"I think perhaps I should go wash my
face. There's so much excitement today. It's
a little stuffy in here, isn't it?"

"I'll crack the door a bit," Tap answered.
As he scurried to the door, he tripped over
the gray and white cat, who let out a squeal
and flew toward the kitchen.

But no one mentioned the cat.

5

Tap was standing in the yard the next morning as Pepper and the McCurleys pulled out. He watched as the rising sun lit the tops of the trees and then crept its way to the ground. He could feel the slight September morning chill start to fade in the light of a cloudless morning. Brownie pranced in the corral, demanding to be ridden. Tap pushed his hat back and sighed as the gray and white cat rubbed his ankle.

"Cat, do you know that six weeks ago I was down in the desert pit, locked behind iron bars? If A.T.P. is Hades, then this is Heaven."

He sauntered back to the house and refilled his coffee cup.

Even the house seems different. Fresh . . . sweet . . . lived in. A man could get used to that — real used to it.

He spent the morning using Onespot to drag the two dead horses away from the barn and into a steep, short ravine, where he caved the dirt in over the top of them.

"I shouldn't have shot those horses. It just caused more problems than I wanted," he muttered to himself as he mounted Brownie and set out to inspect the ranch.

Taking a grub sack stuffed with leftovers from the night before, Andrews rode east up Village Belle Creek toward the crown of the Medicine Bows. At first, the land was rolling and rocky, but otherwise barren. The brown grass of September was thick and obviously ungrazed. Huge white clouds hung like clean sheets on a clothesline strung over the mountains. The sky was a dark blue, and the sun, while bright, didn't produce as much warmth as Tap thought it would. Within an hour he had dug out his jacket and pulled it over his vest.

There's somethin' about this — ridin' over your own ranch, looking at rocks, trees, grass, and a stream that belong to you. It's like comin' home to a place you only knew in your heart. Somehow the saddle's softer, the breeze more tolerable, and every breath of air tastes sweeter.

After reaching a stand of lodgepole pines, Tap turned northeast and followed an animal trail through meadows, trees, and rocks until he came to the summit of the range.

Well, Brownie, as much as I can figure, this is the property line. From here, north to the state line is all ours. If I had a spyglass, I could probably see the ranch house from here. I suppose someday we'll have to stretch some Glidden's wire across this crest. But if we feed the cows down in the valley, they should hang around without wandering too far off. There isn't much of a reason for a bovine to meander up here in the rocks."

The bleat of an animal rolled up the mountain.

"Brownie, that sounds like a cow!"

He rode the horse off the crest and back into the trees. Every few feet he stopped and listened to the bellow of the cow. Dropping down a slight incline, Tap came to the headwaters of another stream, which he guessed was Camp Creek.

He crossed the small creek slowly, as the smooth immersed rocks were thick with dark green moss. Once across, he spurred the horse toward the far side of the meadow that had not yet turned brown. There among the tall weeds and fallen logs he observed a big brown and white bull trying to haul its hind hooves out of a bog. Spotting Andrews and his horse, the bull yanked desperately to extract itself from the mud, but only succeeded in getting the front hooves stuck as well.

"Well, old boy, I don't know where you belong, but it's not there." Circling around to its left hindquarters, Tap spotted an old Rafter R brand barely visible in its hide. "So you're supposed to be up there in Wyoming, are ya? I might as well drive you there. It's right on my way."

Tap jerked his rope off the right side of his saddle while the horse stared at the complaining bull.

"Brownie, let's edge up a little closer and see if I can't toss a lasso over him. That old boy's lookin' weak. There's no tellin' how long he's been stuck."

The runoff from the spring was minimal, which allowed Tap to ride up within twenty-five feet of the animal and still keep Brownie on dry land.

"Now you listen up, horse. I don't know if you're a ropin' mount or not, but you're goin' to learn real soon. I'm sure not goin' to tie him hard and fast. If that old boy gets free and has enough strength to break to the trees, we'd get beat to death on the timbers."

Building a loop in his well-worn fifty-foot hemp rope, Tap stood in his stirrups, circling the coil above his hat. With a skill that takes years to learn and is never forgotten, he floated the rope over the horns of the large animal.

The bull didn't seem to be bothered by the rope, and Tap dallied the other end on the saddle horn. Turning Brownie on an angle away from the spring, he spurred the horse and tugged on the rope. The bull continued to bellow as the rope grew taut.

After several minutes of horse, bull, rope, and rider straining, he slacked up on the rope and rode a bit further north.

"Well, let's try it at a different angle."

This time the violent tugging produced its intended result. The bull lunged, one foot at a time, out of the bog of the springs and onto dry ground. Tap had released the dally and was ready to drop the rope if the animal bolted. Instead, the huge multi-colored longhorn dropped to its knees and collapsed in the grass.

Tap rode close enough to loosen the loop and slip it off the animal.

"Come on now! Don't go down on me. You need to walk this off, or you won't be able to move by mornin'! He-yah! Git up! Git up!" He slapped the now-coiled rope against his chaps and shouted at the animal.

"Come on, bull! Let's go!"

By continual whacking of the coiled rope on the animals rump, he got the bull to struggle to its feet.

"That-a-boy! Keep it goin'!"

The animal staggered a few feet and then stopped to eat some grass.

"Dinner time? Well, I can't argue with you there. But just a little bit. You've got to keep movin' . . . That's enough. Now you move along. Hay-yah! Git on! Git on!"

The bull turned away from the pair, and instead of trotting ahead of them to the north, he spun south and tottered right back out into the bog.

"No! No, you chunkhead! Look at that! You're stuck again!" Tap shouted in frustration. "I'd leave you right there to die, but you'll foul my stream."

Once again he roped the animal and began to tug it out of the morass. This time it took four different angles to finally get the animal to dry land. Again the bull collapsed in the grass.

This time Tap circled behind the animal and positioned himself between the bull and the spring. He gave the bull a few moments to catch his breath.

Slapping his chaps, he hollered, *"Otra vez, el toro! Otra vez!"* Inching the horse forward, he beat on the bull's rump until it staggered to its feet. It glanced to the right, as if to spot the spring for another repeat, but Tap cut the brown horse in that direction, blocking the bull's line of sight.

Suddenly the struggling bull spun and made a pass at Brownie, trying to hook the horse in the right shoulder. Brownie reared and jerked to the left so quickly that Tap found himself slipping over the back of the cantle and tumbling to the ground, with his rope still clutched in his right hand.

His left foot hit a granite rock and twisted until his ankle touched ground, and he staggered back and crashed on his back side. Sitting up quickly, he saw the bull pawing at the ground not fifteen feet from him. Dropping the rope, Tap leaped to his feet to sprint to Brownie, but his left ankle collapsed, slamming him back to the ground. Lying on his left side, Tap yanked his Colt from the holster and fired a shot over the animal's head just as it began to charge. With the next bullet aimed for the bull's head, he pulled back the hammer of the gun. This time the animal suddenly veered off to the left and staggered into a clump of pines.

"On second thought, maybe we'll just leave that old boy up here. If they want him, they can come get him." He motioned to Brownie, who wandered up to Tap once the bull was out of sight.

He stood gingerly on his ankle and hobbled over to grab the reins. Tying his rope back to his saddle horn, Andrews remained on the ground.

"I've got to walk this thing off, or it will stiffen up, Brownie. So come on. Let's find out what other surprises are hidin' on this ranch."

As he walked slowly down a gentle slope, the ankle regained its strength. After about a mile Tap remounted the horse and trotted north.

"Well, we know some of the Rafter R beef got through that drift line. 'Course, that old boy might have been down here for a number of years. Now you'd think that a bull would get awful lonesome and want to go home to visit with the ladies. Unless, of course, he brought the whole harem with him."

He hadn't ridden more than a mile when he spotted a longhorn cow, a yearling, and a calf.

Well, here's the rest of the family, but they aren't branded. Not even the cow! If I ran them back down to the ranch, no one could prove . . . but I don't think that's what Hatcher would have done. No, sir, I'll play it by the book. I'm going to be the perfect neighbor.

It was late afternoon by the time Tap reached the Wyoming border and the edge of Hatcher's ranch. He was pushing ahead of him six longhorn cows (two of which were pregnant), two heifers, three yearlings, and two calves. None of the bunch wore any brand at all. They were skittish about being driven along, but the cows were too close to dropping calves to put up much resistance. Brownie had turned out to be a first-rate cow pony, never allowing any of the herd to stray too far.

"Well, Brownie, it's green down at the bottom of that draw. We'll push 'em down there and then leave 'em. I imagine some of the Rafter R boys will spot 'em in a day or two. It's gettin' late. If we don't get a good moon among these clouds, it might be a long ride home in the dark."

They had ridden halfway down the slope when a rifle shot burned the air near Tap's head, and he heard the report from the trees. He dove for Brownie's neck, shifting to the right side and swinging down, Indian-style. Spurring the pony, he raced toward a buckskin pinc that leaned like a broken flagpole, offering the only shelter besides the trees that housed the attacker.

Reaching the standing dead tree, Tap pulled his Winchester and jumped off the horse, allowing it to wander on down the mountain. Flipping up the long-range sight mounted on the upper tang, he took aim on the trees and waited for someone to show himself.

This is just like Arizona! I've been here two days, and already someone is taking a shot at me! I don't even know anyone in Wyoming, do I? Besides, they can't see from that far away. How do they know who I am?

After a few minutes, Tap saw two riders swing out deep to the left and three start out to the right.

They think they're going to flank me? I'll put one on the ground right now!

He took aim on the one riding a blue roan. The small peep hole centered on the man's chest. He cocked the hammer and began to pull the trigger.

A blue roan? Wiley was ridin' a . . . Wiley? Quail? These are Rafter R boys! And they don't have any idea who I am or whether I'm bringing cattle back or stealin' 'em. That was mighty close, Andrews. If you don't get yourself under control, you may never live long enough to get to that weddin'.

As the men circled in the distance, Tap pulled off his bandanna and tied it to the end of his rifle. *I don't have a white one, but red ought to get their attention.*

He looked up to see a short man and the man on the blue roan swing together toward his position. The others stopped their circling and waited.

"At the buckskin," the little man hollered. "You want to talk before we kill you?"

Andrews knew he could drop both men before they even had a chance to return fire.

That would leave it three to one . . . Think like a Hatcher. You're not John Wesley Hardin . . . and you're not John Wesley.

"Mister, there isn't one chance in a thousand of any of you five gettin' the drop on me. Wiley, is that you on the blue roan?"

The young man sat straight up and pushed his hat back. "Who's calling me out?"

"Tap . . . eh, Tap Hatcher from down on

the Triple Creek Ranch."

"Tap? What in tarnation are you doin' across the state line?"

"Is the mouthy one with you the boss?"

"Eh . . . this is Fightin' Ed Casey. He owns the outfit."

"Tell him to shove the rifle back in the scabbard, and let's talk this out. No reason for men to die today."

"How do we know we can trust you, Hatcher?" Casey yelled.

"I don't trust you for a minute, but I'll trust Wiley. Send him up, and let me give him a message."

"How do I know you won't kill him?" Casey shouted.

"How do you know I won't shoot you right now?" Tap countered. "If Wiley doesn't trust me, he doesn't have to come up."

The two men said something to each other. Then Wiley rode straight up to him.

"Tap, you about got yourself shot."

"Wiley, I hate to mention how long I had you in this peep sight before I figured out who it was. Now, listen, tell good old Fightin' Ed that I found a longhorn bull with an old Rafter R brand, but I couldn't get him talked into goin' home. But I rounded up his family and drove them down here. I'm just bein' neighborly tryin' to help you boys out. Tell him I'm not drivin' them off. I'm bringin' them home."

131

"That ain't the problem, Tap," Wiley replied. "Fightin' Ed is convinced you're workin' for them Boston bankers."

"What?"

"We don't have a longhorn on this whole ranch anymore. Those aren't our cattle."

"But the Rafter R on the bull?"

"Well, you see . . . about five years ago this ranch was owned by an old Scotsman by the name of McGregor who refused to sell out to the Boston bank folks who wanted to search for copper over in those low mountains. But rather than make him a good offer, they had a Denver man sucker him into buyin' two hundred choice longhorns. Well, to make it short, those bovines was infected with Texas fever, and the bank folks knowed it. Within two years the old man lost all his stock except for them longhorns, of course. The ranch went up for sale on the auction block. The bank figured no cattleman would want to take it over, so they made a low offer figurin' to get it fer nothin'. But they got outbid by Fightin' Ed. He comes in, sold off all the longhorns, and lets it stand empty through a hard winter. After that he restocked with polled Herefords. Now he gets plumb agitated if he finds any strangers on the ranch 'cause he figures it's that Boston bank group tryin' to clean him out like they did McGregor."

"So these must be old stock from years

132

ago," Tap offered.

"I reckon so. Must be others up in the Medicine Bows too, but no one wants to mix them in with their own. 'Course, if a man didn't have any cattle at all, he could take 'em and raise 'em. They taste just fine, you know."

"Well, go explain my situation to Fightin' Ed there, and I'll push them right back into my place. I can always eat 'em for dinner. I never thought bein' a good neighbor would get a man in such trouble."

Wiley glanced back at Ed Casey. "Tap, I would never quit a brand before fall roundup, but come next spring if you're lookin' for a hand, let me know. I like workin' cattle, but firin' shots at every stranger who rides on the ranch jist ain't my style."

"I can't promise that I can afford any hands," Andrews admitted. "But your name's on the top of my list, Wiley."

The Rafter R cowboy rode back to Casey, and they had a long talk. All of a sudden, Tap saw the ranch owner pull out his rifle and point the barrel in his direction. He ducked behind the pine just as a shot rang out and splinters flew from the dead pine.

"Hatcher, that Triple Creek Ranch ought to be mine, and you know it!"

Andrews kept himself behind the buckskin pine and leveled his rifle at Casey.

"Wiley, get him out of here, or he's dead. Believe me now, he's a dead man! I'll have these cows off the ranch in thirty minutes, but not with you standin' around takin' pot shots! Get him home, Wiley. I don't plan on waitin' much longer."

"Hatcher . . . you cross that state line again, for any reason, I'll shoot you on sight. Do you hear me?" Casey screamed.

Andrews never took the sight off Casey until he and the others retreated past the clump of trees on down the slope. Working quickly, Tap caught up to Brownie, rounded up the cattle, and drove them back to the Colorado state line.

Other cattle down in those hills? Maybe I'll just go to raising longhorns. But what in the world did Zachariah Hatcher do to make Casey so mad? Obviously they never met. No matter how big the outfit, a guy always wants more land.

He had just crossed over into Triple Creek country when the sun sank and a cold wind blew down from the northwest. He wanted to make it to the ranch by dark, but it was now obvious that would be impossible. He reached a big bend in a stream about dark and abandoned the cattle to the grass next to the water.

"Well, Brownie, I can't believe I came out here without my bedroll. It'll be a slim camp tonight."

He pulled the saddle and tack off the horse, stacking each item back in the cottonwoods. Then he led Brownie out near the stream, watered and hobbled him. After scratching the tall horse's cheek and rubbing his neck, he turned and hiked back to the trees.

A cold drop or two of rain stung his face as he gathered up dead wood for a fire. By the time he had a blaze going, the rain pelted his yellow slicker like buckshot falling from the sky. Sitting cross-legged on his saddle next to the fire, he propped his saddle blanket across his lap. He turned up his collar and screwed his hat, already running water, down tight. With his back to the storm, he dug out a chunk of dry bread and a mass of slightly soaked jerky.

This shouldn't be happening. I've got a house, dry bed, and warm fireplace down off this mountain someplace. What am I doin' up here? I can't believe I left my bedroll in the barn. My whole life spent on the drift, and now I'm caught in a storm like a tenderfoot.

The fire smoked and steamed as it tried to flame above the dampening of the rain. Even with his collar fastened tight, water began to roll down his neck and soak into the shoulders of his jacket and shirt. The saddle blanket was saturated and felt heavy, cold, and wet on his duckings. He could feel water trickling down his leg and soaking his socks. Soon his toes were wet and cold. A shiver slid down his back as he stuffed some more wet meat in his mouth to keep his teeth from chattering. He figured the fire wouldn't last too much longer.

Just a cup of hot coffee. At least I could have toted the coffeepot. It's goin' to be a long night, Andrews. A really long night.

The rain was sporadic, ranging from heavy to light, but it never stopped. It was as persistent as the cold northwest wind that pushed it along.

When the morning sky gave the first hint of gray, Tap found himself dozing off, still propped up on his saddle and soaked to the bone. He could feel the water in his boots. He scouted for dry wood, but found none at all. So, retrieving Brownie, he saddled up wet and turned toward the ranch.

The horse trotted toward the cattle who had spent the night lying in the little meadow next to Camp Creek with their back ends pointed at the storm.

"We don't need to drive 'em, boy. Let's just get home and . . . well, you're right, it would be good to graze them out behind the barn. Okay, we'll push 'em, but if they make a break for it, we're lettin' them run."

Andrews's joints were stiff, and his bones ached from cold. It was a throbbing, dangerous cold that made Tap forget everything but survival. The thought occurred to him that he could be going down the wrong draw and might miss the house altogether. The morning dragged on. Each ridge and draw looked the same. Each felt cold and remote. It was with delight, then, that he crested a ridge and spotted the barn in the distance.

"Brownie, we'll leave 'em right here. I'll put you in the barn, and I'm going to build a big fire and sleep all day." Tap spurred the horse and broke into a trot to cover ground quickly behind the ranch buildings. He tried to keep his teeth from chattering as the rain battered his face and the wind whipped around him. Mud flew from the horses hooves, but he tried to keep his mind on the warm pleasures of a roaring fire.

"Where's your buddy, Brownie?" The black horse was not in the corral. "Well, maybe old Onespot found a way to break into the barn."

Surprised to find the barn door partially open, Andrews glanced around. The sight caused him to leap from the saddle with his Colt drawn.

Scattered in the mud in front of the house were pots, pans, groceries, broken chairs, the ripped mattress, broken tables. Andrews ran into the house through the front door that stood open to the blowing rain.

"No. No," he yelled.

The big living room was stripped of all furnishings except for the wood box. The bedroom was empty except for the built-in dresser. The window in the bedroom was broken. Shards of broken glass, dumped flour, and air-tight cans punctured with bullet holes littered the kitchen floor. All the cupboard doors stood open, and most of the contents had been scattered about the room. The gray and white cat lay sleeping on the top shelf.

"Cat, I hope this didn't inconvenience you too much," he shouted. "Because it's certainly going to torment me."

He grabbed up a fairly clean flour sack from the floor and hiked back out into the storm. Leading Brownie into the barn, he was not surprised to find that the black horse was not there either.

"They stole him, Brownie . . . They stole Onespot, and the storm will wash out any trail." He dragged off the saddle and tack, pulled down some hay into the stall, and then began to rub down the horse with the flour sack.

"We'll get 'em, Brownie, we'll get 'em. It's that Jordan Beckett gang, and they'll pay. Yes, sir . . . they'll pay."

Circling the house and barn twice, Andrews could find no sign of anyone. He sloshed his way back to the house carrying his saddlebags. Within a few minutes he had a fire beginning in the fireplace. Then he went outside and dragged many of the items back into the big main room. Some of the furniture that looked repairable he stacked on the front porch.

My bedroll, blankets . . . everything. They'll be sorry!

Once inside the room, he pulled off his yellow slicker and hung his drenched hat on a peg by the fireplace. Finding no dry clothes or bedding, Andrews had just about resigned himself to stripping down and trying to warm up by the fire. Then his eye caught sight of a short chain hanging from the ceiling in the opposite end of the room from the fireplace.

An attic? There's an attic up there?

Pulling the chain, Andrews lowered a ladder that folded out of the ceiling. He climbed to the top step, glanced into the darkness, and scurried back down the ladder to get a lamp. Lighting it, he carried it ahead of him up the ladder. The attic wasn't tall enough to stand in. It measured about twelve feet by no more than eight feet. Among the assortment of discarded broken furnishings stood a dusty trunk with an old dried-out lantern on top.

He began to sort through the trunk. There were two blankets, a small pillow, a tin with jerky and biscuits petrified beyond all use, a slightly rusted revolver and box of .44 shells, an empty canteen, and there at the bottom a pair of duckings and a worn flannel plaid shirt.

Somebody stashed this up here in case of trouble. Well, this is trouble. The trunk was too awkward to pack, so he tossed the dry goods down to the main room floor. He left the revolver and bullets in the attic.

Within a few minutes, Andrews was dressed in the dry clothing. The green plaid shirt was too narrow in the shoulders and upper arms. But he was delighted to find anything dry. He hung his own clothing about the room and collapsed in front of the fire. Wrapped in the blankets, he rested his head on the rough canvas pillow.

Somewhere in the depth of the most-needed sleep, his mind drifted to the Arizona Territorial Prison in Yuma. He was in a tiny cell . . . The hot, dusty wind swirled off the desert . . . The iron bars blistered his hands . . . The stifling shade at the back of the cell hid unseen stinging bugs . . . His throat was dry . . . He wanted to run down to the Colorado River and plunge beneath its refreshing waters . . . He wanted a cool drink, a soft voice. Red Irma screamed out vulgar obscenities from the women's section, first in English, then in Spanish . . . hour after hour after hour.

He called out to God for deliverance.

No deliverance came.

Now there were scorpions in the cell — scorpions that grew bigger at each glance, scorpions that he could not crush with his boot. He could hear the screaming of other inmates as they received the scorpions venom. He could hear the lewd taunts of Red Irma.

Now in the cell he saw a Gila monster . . . red and black . . . bigger than a small dog . . . It waddled over and grasped his leg. He couldn't move . . . The leg was shackled to the bed . . . A scorpion crawling across the back of his hand lifted its tail to strike.

Tap Andrews was awakened by his own scream.

He found himself sitting up in a dark room in front of glowing coals from a fire. Sweat rolled down his forehead. His shirt collar was drenched. His temples throbbed.

The ranch. I'm not in Arizona.

Tap's back was stiff and ached from sleeping on the hard wooden floor. When he stood to his feet, his left leg cramped, and he couldn't get it straightened out.

He hobbled around in the near-total darkness and found a lantern. Lighting it, he glanced at the gray and white cat sleeping near the fire. Then he went to the front

141

door and stepped to the porch.

It was cold.

Dark.

And clear.

I slept until evenin'?

He took a deep breath. He felt the frigid air in his lungs and the night chill on his wet shirt. He turned back into the house. Digging through the kitchen, he scooped up a couple handsful of coffee from the floor where it had been dumped and tossed them into the coffeepot retrieved from the yard. He hooked it over the iron bar stretched across the front of the fireplace. Then he stirred up the fire, petted the sleeping cat, and changed back into his own now dry clothing.

His head still throbbed as he carried out a lantern and checked on his horse. "Well, Brownie, you get some rest, because we've got a lot of ridin' to do tomorrow."

He spent the next couple of hours scraping things up in the kitchen and trying to return anything still useable to its proper place. The bed turned out to be in fairly good condition, but the leathers were cut. He doubted if the mattress would ever dry out.

Having straightened up what he could, Andrews drank one last cup of coffee. Then he gathered the two blankets and rolled them up in his now-dry bedroll. Tossing his yellow slicker over his shoulder, he picked up his saddlebags, bedroll, and Winchester and hiked over to the barn.

"Partner, it's softer up in that loft than it is in the house. Besides, I wouldn't want nothin' happenin' to you tonight, now would I?"

He spread the bedroll on three feet of hay, crawled under the blankets, left both the Winchester and the Colt, fully loaded and hammers set, next to his right hand.

This time when Andrews fell asleep, he didn't dream at all.

When he awoke, a predawn glow was beginning to lighten the eastern sky. The gray and white cat slept at his feet in the hay.

He toted his dried-out saddle blanket back from the house and got Brownie ready to ride.

"Well, cat, me and Brownie's got work to do. We're going to get Onespot back . . . and we're going to settle this someplace besides my own ranch. You take care of things, ya hear?"

Tap rode south to the mouth of the canyon and then slanted southwest to pick up the main trail north from McCurley's hotel. The sky was a deep September blue, but the air felt cold. He wore his coat buttoned tight and his bandanna wrapped around his neck all day.

Since he had no food with him, there was no reason to stop for dinner. But he did rest the horse from time to time, loosening the cinch and walking the animal.

His thoughts bounced between rage and resignation all day long.

It's always been this way. It doesn't matter if I'm Tap Andrews, or Zachariah Hatcher, or Joe Jones . . . if there's a scrap within five hundred miles, I get sucked into the center of it.

I have no idea what Hatcher would have done in such straits. But I do know what I need to do. No one ever steals a horse from Tap Andrews. Even if I succeed, I may have to move on up the road. Somebody will twist it around, and I'll get the blame.

The sun was low on the western mountains when McCurley's place came into view. He rode Brownie slowly as he approached, studying each horse and buckboard parked in front.

She'll probably be standing at a window looking for me or something. Somehow I've got to tell her about the ranch without it worryin' her to death. She already is frightened about the crowd at Pingree Hill. If I tell her I'm riding in there alone, she'll pitch a fit.

Well, Miss Cedar . . . out here a man can't let someone ride in and steal his horse. We got rules to follow, and if you break the rules, well, you have to pay the penalty. And the penalty for stealin' Onespot is havin' to look down the barrel of Tap Andrews's gun.

Yeah, I'll just explain it to her straight and simple.

She'll understand.

I hope.

It was Bob McCurley who met him on the porch. "Hatcher. I didn't know you were comin' down."

"Well, Bob, I had a little trouble at the ranch and needed to get some supplies."

"Trouble? What happened?"

"They stole Onespot and wrecked up the house pretty good while I was ridin' the property line."

"No."

"I'll need a few supplies. It seems like I'll be taking a trip over to Pingree Hill if you'll scratch me a map."

"That's a rough bunch . . . but I guess you already know that." Bob nodded.

"Yeah . . . well, I better go in and tell Pepper what happened."

"Oh . . . my, well . . . yes, you should, but you can't," McCurley stammered.

"What do you mean I can't?" Andrews pushed his gray hat back.

"She's not here. She's gone."

"Gone?"

"Yep, she borrowed the buggy and left this morning."

6

The trip back to the hotel had been a pleasant one for Pepper. Sitting in the back seat of the buggy, she wore an emerald green suede cape over her shoulders. A neatly folded lap blanket stretched across her legs. The September breeze was cool, but comfortable as long as the occasional rolling clouds didn't block the sun.

Mr. and Mrs. McCurley seem mighty thoughtful. I expect they would make good friends for the Hatchers. I don't suppose they'd feel the same about Pepper Paige, dance-hall girl. It's been a long time, a long time since I've felt this good. Girl, you've just got to make it work. It just might be the only chance you get in this life.

When they reached the hotel, Mrs. McCurley led her up to the room she had used before.

"This will be your home until you and Mr. Hatcher get married," Mrs. McCurley offered.

"Let me pay you something in advance." Pepper reached for her purse which contained most of Suzanne Cedar's inheri-

147

tance. She handed her a twenty-dollar green-back.

"Well, that will take care of things for several weeks. Now if you want to talk, just come down and look me up. I'll probably be stuck down in the kitchen most of to-day."

Pepper fidgeted around in her room — sitting . . . standing . . . pacing . . . looking in the mirror . . . staring out the window. She kept worrying about what was happening to Zachariah Hatcher.

I need to be there. What if he finds out about me, and I don't have a chance to explain? What if he learns what happened over at Pingree Hill? What if Abel Cedar rides in? What if Jordan Beckett shows up? If he and the others come back, they'll kill him.

He did take care of himself rather neatly though. You wouldn't think a man like Mr. Hatcher would have that much gun savvy. He probably has other surprises, too.

Of course, I have a few surprises for him.

Boy, do I have some surprises!

Borrowing some stationery from Mrs. McCurley, Pepper spent part of the morning composing a letter to the Wemberly Hotel in Fort Collins, instructing them to forward the trunks and other personal belongings of Suzanne Cedar to the McCurley Hotel.

She washed her one simple dress that she'd worn for the past two days and hung it in her room to dry. She took dinner in her room and borrowed some sewing supplies from Mrs. McCurley. Sitting by the north window of her room, able to see if anyone rode in from the direction of Hatcher's ranch, she began to alter one of her dance-hall dresses. Taking some material from a black dress that was too risque for redemption, she lengthened the dress, altered it to hang straight down, and reworked the bodice. Borrowing some lace from another dress, she attached a lace collar and made a shawl. Finally completing the renovation, she modeled the dress in front of the mirror.

Pepper, you can sew. You should have been a seamstress . . . instead of runnin' off with a travelin' man like Jeremiah McCabe — a man so reckless as to get himself killed in the first town we landed in. Why, you could be married to some bank clerk, livin' in some little shack in Boise City, growin' six barefoot kids, and havin' to take in laundry.

She stared intently at the eyes reflecting back at her from the mirror and then broke into a grin.

Which, of course, is why you are right here today.

She wore the altered dress to supper and was pleased by the comments of those in the dining room. A well-dressed man wearing a black tie and a long coat sat down across the table from her.

"Miss Cedar, we haven't met . . . but I learned your name from Bob McCurley. My name is Shelby Lindermann."

"Pleased to meet you, Mr. Lindermann," she acknowledged. "What brings you to McCurley's? If you will forgive me, you look a little overdressed for this area."

"Yes, you're quite right about that. Well, I work for a Boston banking group that's interested in investing in western land. Specifically, in mining concerns."

"Oh, my, do you mean there is some valuable ore in this district?"

"Well, that's what we don't know yet. I'm just gathering information. If it looks promising, we'll send out our team of geologists. Say, I've heard you came from the East."

"I wouldn't call it the East. I just came out here from Chicago, but Kentucky is my home."

"Well, I worked several years in Chicago. Which part of town did you live in?"

"Oh, I never really lived there. . . ." Pepper glanced around the table hoping to find a way to change the subject. "My mother just moved up, and I stopped by to visit on my way west."

"Which part of town does your mother live in?"

"Eh . . . you know, by the . . . on the

150

north side . . . I think. I really don't know my way around there very well."

"On the north side? Probably has one of those lovely homes near the lake. Well, I should have known by your demeanor that you had that kind of heritage. Listen," Lindermann leaned across the table and spoke in a hushed tone, "I don't mean to sound patronizing, but most folks in the West are so — so simple in mind and manner. Your charm really does stand out. As I'm sure you must know, you are a strikingly handsome woman."

"Why, thank you, Mr. Lindermann!"

You pompous prig! Do you think for a minute I don't know what you're after? I've been faking a smile at your type all my life. Why don't you invite me up to your room for some imported wine and a discussion of French impressionistic painters? It would be a delight to slap your pasty-lookin' face just to see the shock in your eyes.

"Perhaps after supper you would enjoy a stroll around the premises? I do enjoy a brisk walk after the evening meal," he continued with a wry smile. "It's one of life's special pleasures, especially when accompanied by such a lovely lady. I find the fresh air clears my mind and helps me make better decisions."

A walk in the woods? Oh, sure. Just to talk about mining claims, no doubt. Any

151

particular decisions that involve me?

"Why, thank you, sir, but I'm afraid I must decline. I have more plans to make for my upcoming wedding," she replied with a charming fake lilt to her voice.

"Oh . . . ah . . . wedding?" Lindermann glanced around the room. "I, eh . . . didn't know. None of the men told me. Eh, is your fiancé here at the hotel?"

"No," she laughed, "I'm fearful if he were here, you'd be looking down the barrel of a cocked .44. I'm afraid he's rather protective, you know. But don't let it keep you awake listening to night noises. Why, with any luck he'll never hear about you makin' a pass at me."

"Oh! My! I didn't think I was . . . I mean, I didn't . . . did I? No . . . no offense intended, I assure you," he stammered.

"And no offense taken." She nodded.

Lindermann, looking visibly shaken, quickly excused himself from the table. She sat staring at his empty chair.

Maybe I overreacted. I mean, he wasn't going after Pepper Paige, dance-hall girl, but he was addressing Miss Suzanne Cedar. Maybe it's sort of what they do . . . I suppose he could have been on the square. Pepper, you don't think they're all a bunch of lyin', cheatin', unreliable woman-chasers. What would Miss Cedar have done?

After a final cup of coffee, she excused

herself from the table and walked out to the veranda at the front of the hotel. Mr. Lindermann sat on the bench smoking a pipe and watching the declining western sun.

"Mr. Lindermann? May I have a word with you?"

"Oh . . . certainly, Miss Cedar." He nodded, removing the pipe from his lips and nervously looking around the yard.

"Well . . . I just felt like perhaps I came across rather coldly with my comments at the supper table. I suppose I was acting as if you were one of . . . well, I could have been more polite. Forgive my effrontery."

"Certainly, Miss Cedar. And no apology is needed. There are times in the West when I forget certain rules of civility."

"The rules are different out here, aren't they?" Pepper added.

"Yes, indeed. They seem to be enforced in a more definitive, personal manner. But I believe you understand them better than I."

"Well . . . that might be so. Will you be going on that walk now?" she asked.

"I believe I will, if you promise there will not be a jealous fiancé hiding in the trees with a pistol drawn."

"Oh, no. He's back at our . . . I mean, at his ranch."

"Well, what is this lucky fellow's name?"

"Zachariah Hatcher. He owns —"

"The Triple Creek Ranch up on the state line, correct?"

"Why, yes. Do you know Tap?"

"Tap?"

"Oh, it's just a nickname."

"Well, actually, no, I've never met the man. But it's my business to know who owns land in the area in case my employers want to purchase property for mining exploration. So I keep up on all sales and claims in the district."

"Do you mean there might be gold up on the ranch?"

"I have no indication of any valuable minerals in that area, but one never knows what might be discovered in the future. There is some copper not too far away, and it might stretch down to the Triple Creek area."

"Well, wouldn't that be somethin' . . . er, something?"

"I was wondering," Mr. Lindermann asked, "where are you and Mr. Hatcher going to have your wedding? I haven't heard of a church in this sector."

"Oh, there's none around close. So we'll have a service at the ranch."

"When is the big date?"

"That's a good question," she acknowledged. "According to the McCurleys, a Reverend passes through here every couple of months. We'll have him do the honors."

"Reverend? All you need is a Reverend?"

"Why, yes. You aren't a clergyman, are you?"

"Me? Heavens no! But I was just down at Jack Rand's place. There was a traveling parson — Methodist, I believe — visiting some families in the area. Perhaps he could . . . but I do believe he was headed toward Fort Collins."

"Maybe he'll be coming by here!" Pepper flashed.

"Well . . . perhaps. But he said he needed to be in Fort Collins by next week. I would suppose that means going up to Pingree Hill and then taking the river road, wouldn't you?"

"Oh, no!" she moaned.

"I beg your pardon?"

"Oh . . . I mean, I don't know this country very well yet. But I came through Pingree Hill on the stage not too long ago. Why would the Reverend go there?"

"A large number of folks who could use some religion live around there, I suppose. There's a dive there called April's, and I've heard . . . well, I wouldn't even mention to a lady of your sensibilities the things that I've heard about the women who work there," Lindermann lectured.

"Thank you very much for the information about the Reverend. Do you happen to know his name? Perhaps I could send word to him."

"Houston. I believe it was Rev. Houston. But I'm not sure how you can reach him before he gets to Fort Collins."

"Perhaps you're right, but I will certainly try. Good evening, Mr. Lindermann."

She spun on her heels and retreated into the dining room. Finding Bob McCurley talking to a man with a very bushy beard, she hesitated, took a deep breath, and then marched over to where they were standing.

Slipping her arm into McCurley's, she smiled at the other man. "Bob, I apologize for this interruption, but I must talk to you immediately." Then turning to the other man, she curtsied and smiled widely. "With your permission, may I borrow Mr. McCurley for a few minutes?"

The bearded man nodded. "Why certainly, missy. Me and Bob was just tryin' to outlie each other anyway. I've been tellin' him that Bill Hickok could have outshot any man alive, but he said that he saw some old boy north of here go face to face with five of Beckett's men and never taste lead. Well, I never —"

"You're a real gentleman," she interrupted.

"Oh, yeah. And I'm handsome and rich," he bellowed with a gold-toothed grin and took his coffee cup back for a refill.

"Mr. McCurley," Pepper quizzed, "how can I get a message to a Rev. Houston who's down at Jack Rand's headin' up to Fort Collins?"

"The Reverend? He's in the area? Why, that is good news! But there's nothin' between Rand's and Fort Collins except for a few ranches and that riffraff at Pingree Hill."

"If I were to ride over there, could I intercept him before he gets to Pingree?"

"Oh . . . I suppose it could be done, but it ain't the kind of ride for a lady like yourself. Perhaps you could send a note to Pingree Hill. 'Course, that all depends on how quick someone gets there."

"Is there a trail over to Jack Rand's?"

"Not from here, there ain't. A person would have to cut over the mountains cross-country and pick up the road."

"Can I borrow a horse?"

"You don't aim to ride that by yourself, do you?"

"Yes. I'm not going to sit around for several months waiting to see if a parson saunters by. Mr. McCurley, I assure you, I can succeed."

"Well . . . Miss Cedar, I believe you could. But why don't you send out to Hatcher and have him locate the Reverend? Now there's a man who can handle himself."

"Mr. McCurley, do you have a horse I can borrow or not?" she repeated.

"I don't suppose I could talk you out of it?"

"I certainly doubt it."

"Well, would you like to try it in a buggy? I'm not sure you could cross the mountains, but you could take it to Pingree Hill and then start south toward Rand's ranch."

"I would rather have a sure-footed horse if you have one available."

"You can have a horse, but I sure do wish you wouldn't try this alone."

"Some tasks are meant to be done by yourself. If I can't do any more than hide in a ranch house, then perhaps this is not the country for me. I need to prove to myself that I can survive in this wild and reckless land."

"What time do you want the horse saddled?"

"If it's not raining, I'd like to leave at daybreak."

"I got a feeling Mr. Hatcher ain't goin' to like me lettin' you go off like this."

"Mr. McCurley, in case you had not noticed, I didn't ask your permission."

"No, ma'am, you didn't. I'll have the horse ready."

"Thank you very much. I will be ready to ride."

"If it don't rain," McCurley added.

"Yes, yes . . . provided it don't rain."

It poured all that night and most of the next day. Pepper wasted the hours standing by her second-story window, looking at the road to the north, watching drops of water glide down the glass pane in front of her.

If Mr. Hatcher comes to town today, he will insist on going to find the Reverend. He'll end up at Pingree Hill, and someone will tell him about me. I must get out and find the Reverend first, 'cause if the parson gets to Pingree, they'll tell him about the young lady who died.

First, we must get married. Then later, after we're situated, after everything settles in . . . maybe after we have a baby, then, well, then I'll tell Tap the truth. Oh, he'll be shocked at first, but I'll make sure he is in no way disappointed.

I must leave in the morning no matter how bad the weather might be.

It was still very dark in her room when Pepper woke up and stared upward, trying to focus on her ceiling. She had purposely pushed back the curtains after she turned off the lamp the previous night so that the morning daylight might awaken her. But it was not daylight. The sheets felt cold at her feet, but the big bed was so soft and comfortable she didn't want to get up.

Ranch wives get up early to . . . eh, feed the chickens or milk the cows or gather the eggs or something. Will Tap expect me to get up early? Maybe we shouldn't have a bed this comfortable. My bed at Pingree Hill was so lumpy I had a backache by morning. I don't want a lumpy bed.

With her hands she reached up from under the covers and combed back her blonde hair with her fingers.

Why does Miss Suzanne Cedar always have to pin her hair up? Why can't she just let it blow in the breeze like a little girl? Someday . . . someday I'm going to wear comfortable clothes and let my hair down. I'm goin' to say, "World, this is Pepper Paige, and . . ." I mean, I'll say, "This is Pepper Hatcher, and you better like me the way I am!" Pepper Hatcher? That sounds horrible. Maybe I should have Tap call me Suzanne after all.

She folded the covers back, slipped her wool-stocking-covered feet onto the cold hard wood floor, and felt her way over to the lamp. The bedroom filled with glowing light. Closing the curtains, she shuffled over to the wash basin on the dresser and poured some water into the bowl.

As she washed, she stared into the mirror.

It ain't been an easy life, old girl, has it? No, ma'am. But you're doin' okay now. You bring that parson back, and you could have a wedding in a day or two. You ride out and find him today no matter what.

She dressed methodically, and warm, checking out each layer of clothing in the mirror as she pulled it on.

I will wear my plain brown dress and my simplest hat. Perhaps I will remove the feather — especially if it's raining. I can wear my cape and my long coat. I could borrow an umbrella, but not horseback . . . Well, perhaps I could. Oh, it cain't rain — not today, Lord, not today.

For a split second Pepper thought about praying . . . but instead, she mumbled to herself, "Girl, you ain't prayed since your mama died. He didn't answer you then. He sure ain't goin' to answer you now."

She opened the curtains to reveal the first light of dawn and then sorted through the contents of her large handbag. The money was still there, as were several personal items and her small revolver. Several extra bullets were scattered about the bottom of the bag.

Walking down the curving staircase, she could smell breakfast cooking in the kitchen. Seeing no one in the parlor or dining room, she stepped to the front porch just as Bob McCurley drove a small one-seat carriage to the front of the hotel.

The early morning chill cooled her cheeks and hands. Pepper dug into her bag and pulled out some gloves.

"Can you saddle me a horse now, Mr. McCurley?"

"Nope."

"But I told you I would need one first thing today."

"Now, missy, you can't go ridin' out through these rain-slick hills on a pony. It ain't ladylike, no matter how good a horsewoman you might have been back east. Besides, the only way over to that Reverend after a storm is to take the road to Fort Collins. When we get to Pingree Hill, we can check to see if the Reverend has made it that far. If he ain't, we'll turn toward Jack Rand's place. If he's already been there, we'll chase him down even if we have to go to Fort Collins."

"We? What do you mean, we?" she demanded.

"Oh, Mrs. McCurley and me has been discussin' it, and we decided we couldn't send you out in this weather with all the dangers around. I'm goin' to drive you wherever you want."

"Oh, no," she groaned. "I must do it myself."

"What kind of man would I be — sending you out into this?"

Sure. That's all I need — having the McCurley's find out from April who I really am. I won't go there with anyone from over here — ever!

"You aren't sending me anywhere. I'll be fine with the team. You will rent them to me, won't you?"

"Rent? I ain't rentin' them. If you take this buggy, it's on me. But I don't think you understand the dangers."

"Mr. McCurley, I understand the danger much more clearly than you imagine. I appreciate your concern, but I insist that I go alone, as I already mentioned."

"Well, I figured you'd say that, so I had the missus pack you a dinner in a basket. And I've laid out a couple of lap quilts there for ya. Now I hope you ain't offended, but there's a short little ten-gauge shotgun layin' on the floorboard. You just pump it once, and it's ready to fire. Have you ever shot one of them?"

"More times than I'd like to admit," she acknowledged. "You know — hunting back in Kentucky."

Within a matter of minutes she had the one-horse buggy rolling out of the yard and up the winding road that led eventually to Fort Collins. She soon found that if she sat in the very middle of the seat, she was fairly safe from the mud that flew from the wheels, but that position made her susceptible to whatever was flung off the horses hooves. The only remedy she found was to sit in the middle and drive the horse slowly.

Mr. McCurley had drawn a map to Rand's

ranch, either by going to Pingree Hill or by taking another slower route. He also mentioned several families who might put her up for the night since it wasn't possible to return in one day.

For several miles she bounced along, getting a feel for the rig. After a while she arrived at an understanding with the horse, who would go at a pleasant pace and then begin to veer to the right when he was tired and wanted a rest.

She hoped she would meet no one along the way, but she knew that was an impossibility. The few riders who passed her just tipped their hats and rode on.

As they should do to any respectable rancher's wife, like myself. Well . . . almost his wife.

Pepper had convinced herself that she would take the slower route no matter how much longer it took. But by the time she rested the horse and ate her noon meal, she knew that she had to hurry to Pingree and determine whether the Reverend had passed through yet.

Danni Mae or Stack or someone will come to the porch, and I'll ask them without even getting out of the buggy. I'll need no more than a minute to figure it out.

The muddy road slowed her pace dramatically, and she was surprised that it was getting dark when she came down the grade and saw April's Pingree Hill Dance Hall & Elegant Saloon come into view. She wished she were back in her warm, clean room at the McCurley Hotel, or even better, tucked away in her own home out at the Triple Creek Ranch. Some people named Kasdorf had a place several miles south on the road to Rand's ranch, and the McCurleys had assured her they would be happy to put her up for the night.

She stopped the rig a mile before the dance hall and picked up the cold shotgun. After rechecking the chamber for a shell, she laid it on her lap between the two blankets.

Taking a deep breath, she slapped the reins and drove the team as close to the dance hall as the horses at the hitching rail would allow. The piano rang above the laughter and shouts. No one came to the door or seemed to notice her presence.

After several awkward moments, two men covered with mud from what looked like a long ride rode in from the east and pulled up at the end of the rail.

"Excuse me, could I have a word with one of you?" Pepper called.

The younger of the two strutted across the wooden porch in front of April's, purposely banging his heels and ringing the jinglebobs on his spurs. He tipped his dark hat back, revealing a white forehead above a dirty, unshaven face.

"Well, now, miss, if you're lookin' for a, ah, dancin' partner, you couldn't find no one better than Tobiah Maxwell!"

"And I suppose you are Tobiah Maxwell?"

"Yes, ma'am, now if you'll just let my pard' park that buggy, I'd be more than happy to acquaint you with the delights of this establishment."

"Do you seriously think I look like the type of woman who would enter such a place as this?" Pepper raged.

"Eh . . . well, I thought you reminded me of . . . but, eh, no, ma'am, I reckon you don't. What was it you wanted?"

"I believe there is a piano player by the name of Stack Lowery inside. Would you please go ask him to step out here for a minute?"

The other man walked up to his side and gave Pepper a look. "Ain't I seen you before?" he asked.

"Most assuredly you have not!" she insisted.

Looking up and down the road, the man grinned, exposing tobacco-stained teeth. "You know, we have ways of convincing you to come inside." He leered.

Pepper pulled back the top blanket revealing the shotgun to the startled men.

"Yes, and if you try one of them, you will find yourself with a hole the size of a plate somewhere between your heart and your knees. Is that clear?"

"Eh . . . yes, ma'am, I'll get the piano player," the younger one stammered. "Come on, Boyd, this place is full of easy girls. Ain't no reason to wrestle with a shotgun!"

Both men turned and went inside. In a few minutes she heard the piano cease, but the shouts and laughter continued. Then Stack Lowery stepped out the door.

"Miss Pepper! . . . Or is it Miss Cedar?"

"Miss Cedar, thank you."

"Is everything going according to plan?"

"Well . . . yes, actually, it is. Listen, Stack, I'm over here to find out if a Reverend has passed through here in the past couple of days. I need him to come over and do the weddin' for us."

"You really gettin' married, Pepper?"

"Yeah. Isn't that wild?"

"Do you like him?"

"Who?"

"That rancher. The one you're going to marry. Does he treat you good?"

"Stack, Tap's really a nice man, and I like him very much. He doesn't treat me rough at all. 'Course, I don't know him much yet. But I need to know about a Reverend."

"Well, I just got back late last night myself. So I'll have to ask. Let me check with April."

"Don't tell her I'm out here. I'm not interested in visitin' with nobody."

"Well, she's bound to see you sittin' out here in the open. Why don't you drive it over behind DiCinni's barn? I'll nose around and meet you there. Did you hear about Selena?"

"Did she run away?"

"No, but I guess a night or so after you left, Jordan Beckett came in here all fired up about someone shootin' his horses. Some punchers started grindin' on him about how a dance-hall girl buffaloed him the other night. Well, he was lookin' for you, threatenin' to settle the score. When he found out you was gone, he went crazy shootin' up the place. I knowed I should never have left Miss April.

"Well, I guess he picked out Selena for a dance and gets kind of rough. He was twistin' her arm and tearin' her dress. The others were afraid to stop him. She got where she wouldn't take it no more and pulls a knife on him. He gained a couple of new scratches, and suddenly he just busted her across the face with his fist. She got pretty well beat up before the boys could pull him off. Yeah, Miss Pepper, I surely wish I would have been here!"

"Stack, it isn't your fault there are jerks around like Jordan Beckett."

"Listen, Miss Pepper, it's almost sundown. You'll need a place to stay for the night. How about me slipping you in the back door. You could hole up in my room. I can sleep out in the saloon."

"Stack, do you know some people named Kasdorf that live south of here?"

"I believe so."

"Well, that's where I'm going to spend the night."

"That's good. I didn't know they was friends of yours. They seem like sort of the religious type."

"They are friends of the McCurleys."

"Oh . . . sure. Of course, that would be a mighty fine place to stay. Now pull over there, and I'll see what I can find out. What was that feller's name?"

"I believe it was Rev. Houston — a Methodist. But I'll take any clergyman you can find. It doesn't matter much to me. I don't know one from another."

Stack reentered the dance hall, and Pepper drove the buggy behind the barn that served mainly as a livery for the dance hall and saloon. Seeing no one around, she let the horse drink at the trough and then climbed down and pulled some hay down for the horse. She peeked around the barn to see if Stack was headed her way. He wasn't. She climbed back on the buggy seat, opened the dinner basket, and pulled out a strawberry-jammed biscuit.

She was starting to get quite cold when she heard footsteps coming toward the barn. She slipped her hands under the blanket and clutched the shotgun.

"Miss Pepper?" Stack's familiar voice rang out. "Miss Cedar?" He came around the corner. Listen, I learnt that Rev. Houston is down at Jack Rand's place, but should be headin' this way. April sent word down to him that a woman died and didn't have a proper buryin'. She's hopin' he'll stop by and do the honors."

"That's good news!"

"About him havin' a proper service for that Cedar girl?"

"No. About him not havin' passed by yet. I'll latch on to him first with any luck. He might not make it to Pingree Hill at all. Thanks, Stack. You're one of the few friends I've got in this world."

"Well, you be careful. And stay far away from Beckett. He's plumb mean. He's crazy. He's sayin' you double-crossed him, so he's lookin' for ya."

"I can take care of myself."

"Yes, ma'am, I reckon you can. If a Reverend comes by, I'll send him down to Kasdorfs'."

It was close to dark as she drove south on the road toward the ranches. Unlike the river road from Pingree Hill to Fort Collins, this southern route was little more than two muddy wagon ruts. Pepper began to grow frightened about getting the rig stuck and was delighted to spot smoke rising from a chimney of a large stone house at the end of a wood-fenced drive.

This has got to be the Kasdorfs'.

By the time she rolled up to the front of the house, it was dark. Pepper was cold and tired. Her face felt dirty and her hands grimy. A short, bald man in a bulky sweater came out of the house carrying a lantern in one hand and a rifle in the other.

"Yeah? What do you want?" he called. "Who is there?"

"Are you Mr. Kasdorf?"

"Ya. Who is asking this?"

"Mr. Kasdorf, my name is . . . eh, Suzanne Cedar. I'm a friend of Bob and Mrs. McCurley. They suggested that if I need some overnight accommodations, you might have a spare room."

"Woman, are you by yourself?"

"Eh . . . yes, sir."

"Well . . . well . . . why certainly, you may spend the overnight with us. Come in, come in. I'll take care of your rig in a few minutes. We were just sitting down at the table for supper, and you can join us."

"Thank you, Mr. Kasdorf. I'm much obliged not to have to stop up at Pingree Hill."

"Pingree Hill? That place was invented by the devil himself! Would you mind staying upstairs with our girls? We have a special guest for the evening, and the sofa has already been pledged for the night."

"Whatever you have will be fine." Pepper could feel the stiffness and exhaustion of hours of bouncing in the buggy. "How old are your girls?"

"Fourteen, twelve, and eight. We lost one."

"Oh . . . I didn't know."

"Well, follow me." He led her through the big heavy door on the stone house across a well-swept floor to a separate dining room.

"Look, everyone," he called, "we have more company for supper — a friend of the McCurleys! Mama, you set a plate while she washes up."

"Hi, my name is Rebecca," a small girl greeted her. "Do you work at Pingree Hill?"

"Rebecca! What a horrid thing to say!" Mrs. Kasdorf blushed.

"But she's so pretty, and the ladies down there must be pretty because so many men want to go down there."

"Please forgive my disrespectful daughter," Mr. Kasdorf apologized. "This is Miss Suzanne Cedar. Miss Cedar, I'd like you to meet my wife, Anna, and our daughters

Rachel, Ruth, and Rebecca. And I don't know if you've met before — this is our other guest, Rev. Houston."

7

Tap left Brownie at McCurley's and borrowed two fresh horses. He had one saddled up and was ready to leave the hotel when Bob McCurley came out carrying a lunch sack and a steaming hot cup of coffee.

"Hatcher, you sure do look like you need some rest. She'll be over at the Kasdorfs' by now. Why not ride out in the mornin'?"

"Bob, I've got a sickenin' feelin' that somethin' bad is goin' to happen. It's kind of like when a little rock tumbles off a cliff, but you know it will be a landslide before it reaches bottom. I just got to get out there and see what I can do."

"Well, if you mean goin' up against those that tore up your place, you better let me grab a scattergun and ride along."

"I know this sounds reckless, but I'm goin' to take care of this by myself."

"You two are the stubbornest, most independent, self-confident pair I've ever run across!"

"Two of us?"

"You and that Cedar woman — I cain't talk sense into her either. Why, the two of you will either end up ownin' half the state or takin' pot shots at each other. I swear, you are two of a kind!" McCurley turned and stomped back into the hotel.

Within minutes Tap was riding an ever-darkening trail east, leading his second horse and eating a piece of bread folded over a thick slice of juicy ham.

Although his clothing was completely dried out, he still felt cold. By the time it was dark, he had dug a blanket out of his bedroll and draped it around his shoulders.

Bob claimed this was his best night horse. He's a smooth rider. Maybe I should have slept a few hours. I surely thought owning a ranch would be a whole lot more peaceful than this.

After I get things settled in Pingree Hill, I'll find her and . . . What is she doin' ridin' out here by herself? It's foolhardy and irresponsible. You'd think a woman of Miss Cedar's sensibilities . . . 'Course, comin' out west to marry someone you've never met and only wrote a half-dozen letters to is sort of foolhardy and irresponsible.

Tap, there's a whole lot about that gal that you don't know one blamed thing about. Are you sure you know what you're gettin' into?

Suddenly he laughed out loud. "Tap, you've never known what you were gettin' into, have you?"

The night was still, clear, and increasingly cold. He passed one stage and a couple of riders early in the evening. After that there was no one on the road. About midnight he pulled off and built a small fire. After ten minutes of warming up, he saddled the second horse, kicked out the fire, and remounted, holding the lead rope of the first horse. Even his worn elkskin gloves felt stiff and cold.

"Well, pony, you're a little shorter and a little thinner, but I sure hope you can see at night like your buddy here. You remind me of that little mount I had down in Lincoln. Garrett was chasin' Bonny, and I needed to get down to Las Cruces to see Carmen . . . Or was it Carmelita? . . . It all seems like a long, long time ago."

Rotating horses and dozing as he rode, Andrews arrived at the top of the grade leading down to Pingree Hill right before daylight. Dismounting, he stuffed his blanket back into his bedroll. He could see only one flickering light at the dance hall — and no sign of movement at any of the other buildings.

I wouldn't exactly call this a town. More like a hideout with a road runnin' through it.

Swinging off the main road, he circled behind some trees and came up to a corral and barn across from the dance hall. He tied the horses off in the trees behind the barn and resat the saddle on the freshest mount.

"Just in case I'm in a hurry to leave, you're the one to do it, old boy!" He rubbed the sorrel gelding's neck and then slapped him once on the rump.

Pulling off his saddlebags, he threw them across his shoulder and walked around to the corral of horses. Tap stood by the fence waiting for daylight to shine on the ponies that pranced in the pen. His eyes danced from sorrel, to bay, to grulla, to paint, to black . . . one black . . . two blacks . . . then one with a short white blaze on its nose.

"Onespot?" he murmured. Checking the animal's left thigh, he noticed a circle Mc brand. "That's him!"

Tap slowly sauntered toward the back door of the largest building in the settlement. A place called April's Pingree Hill Dance Hall & Elegant Saloon.

Elegant? Yeah, I'll bet. That means you can't spit on the floor, and you don't have to drink out of the same glass as the puncher next to you.

He was two steps lower than the doorway when he knocked. The man who came to the door seemed to tower over him.

"You want somethin', mister?"

"I know it's early, but I was wonderin' if I could buy a meal? Been ridin' most the night, and I'm hungry. I've got the coin for it."

"This ain't no chop house, you know!" the tall man boomed.

A woman's voice called from back inside the kitchen, "Who's out there, Stack?"

"Some drifter wants to buy breakfast."

"Well, take a dollar and feed him. I'm going upstairs."

"Yes, ma'am — Miss April." Turning to Tap, he held the door open. "You caught her in a generous mood. Come on in. I was stirrin' up a few eggs for myself."

"Generous? You call a one-dollar breakfast generous?"

The big man gave him a grin as wide as his face. "Anything you get for a dollar in this place is a pretty good buy, mister. This happens to be the most expensive place in town."

"Town? It's the only place in town."

"That just proves my point."

The kitchen was small and had a long, narrow wooden table along the east side near the back door. Tap could hear no noise in the place except for the crackle of the wood stove and the snap of frying eggs. The smell of breakfast, next to a pretty woman's perfume, was Tap's favorite aroma.

"My name's Stack. What can I call you?"

"Tap."

178

The big man looked back at him . . . then continued his cooking. "You should stick around 'til evening. This place gets lively. Some real fancy girls work here, and the likker is almost drinkable."

Tap grinned and surveyed what part of the deserted bar and dance hall he could observe through the doorway.

Beckett's boys could be sleepin' it off in the bar . . . or maybe upstairs. They're not the type to have a place of their own.

"Well, I'll have to move on down the road sooner than that. But I would like to buy another horse."

"Don't rightly know if there are any around for sale," Stack responded.

"How about that black with the star on its nose? I'd sure like to have that one."

"I hope you like these well done." He handed Tap a plate of eggs. "That one is pretty new here, but I believe it belongs to Jordan Beckett. Or, at least, to one of his friends. But just between you and me, Beckett's been on the prowl lately. I wouldn't do no horse-tradin' with him in such a nasty mood. Help yourself to some coffee, bacon, and bread." He motioned to the table.

"Is Beckett here?" Tap questioned. "Maybe I could talk to him real careful."

"Nah, he's not here. Don't expect him back too soon neither. He sort of outlived

179

his welcome. After what he done . . ." Stack hesitated as both men heard footsteps approach the kitchen.

Tap reached for his coffee with his left hand while letting the right one settle on the grip of his revolver. A young woman with bark-black hair shuffled into the kitchen wearing a multicolored silk robe. She looked startled to see Tap. He noticed a bruise on her neck and a blackened right eye.

She's been cryin'. What in the world happened?

"Stack, I didn't know we had company," she choked out in a raspy voice.

"Jist a feller eatin' some breakfast, Selena."

Tap glanced back down at his breakfast.

"That's okay, mister, I know I'm a sight," Selena told him, "and if these two loose front teeth fall out, I'll be even worse. I'm goin' to kill him, Stack. I'm going to sneak up when he's passed out from drinkin', and I'll slit his throat from ear to ear — yes, I will!"

"Who?" Tap asked.

"Beckett. He done that to her."

Andrews felt his neck and face flush with anger. He had always operated under a code that some deeds forfeit a man's right to life. Beating up women was high up on Tap's list.

"You mean to tell me he beat on this lady,

180

and you didn't bust his head open?"

"I weren't here, mister. That's the rub. I was away buyin' supplies. But this old boy runs with a gang of five or six. I can't take them all on at the same time."

Andrews could see Selena staring at him. Finally she spoke, *"¿Cómo se llama?"*

"Tap."

"¿Qué?"

"Tapadera. *¿Comprende?"*

"Sí. ¿Por qué no vino la semana pasada?" She flashed an obviously painful smile.

"Porque no sabía que aquí trabajaran mujeres tan hermosas."

"Now you two cut me in on this," Stack protested. "What have you been discussin', or is it too private to tell?"

"We have just been lyin' to each other in order to make us feel better, right, mister?"

"Selena, if I had come through the country last week, you would have been the one I danced the night with."

"Yeah, that sounds nice to my ears." She walked over and grabbed a cup of coffee and then headed back toward the stairs. "If he would have been here last week, that blonde witch would have stole him, right, Stack?"

"Blonde witch?"

"Oh, just one of the girls who quit a few days ago," Stack hurried to explain.

"So you don't know when this Beckett might be back?"

"Nope, but he's got to pick up his horses. It could be he comes right up to the front door, or maybe he'll slip into the corral at night and drive them off. But he won't show up alone. A couple of his boys is carrying lead, but they'll all be here anyway. Beckett don't travel except with a gang. I don't think April will allow them in the door."

"You mind if I hang around and wait to see him?"

"You really want that horse that bad?"

"Yep."

"Well, you can't stay in here. This is for customers only. But there ain't no harm in you hanging out around the barn. You put your horse in the woods?"

"Eh . . . yeah. How'd you know?"

" 'Cause that's what I'd do if I were you. You ain't really plannin' on buyin' that horse, are you, mister?"

"Well . . . no, actually . . ."

Stack motioned him outside. "I'll walk you out to the barn. Bring your coffee if you want."

Once outside Tap glanced up at the big man. "What's this all about?"

"Didn't want none to hear inside. You're Hatcher, ain't ya?"

"You know me?"

"Ain't met you but . . . well, a lady in a

buggy came through here last night, and she happened to mention a rancher by the name of Tap Hatcher."

"Miss Cedar? She was here? Why?"

"Lookin' for a parson."

"Where did she go?"

"Well, she was headed down the road south to some folks called Kasdorf. But if she didn't find the Reverend there, she was going to ride all the way to Jack Rand's place. That's a good twenty-five or thirty miles away."

"Thanks, Stack. I'm glad to hear that she's safe."

"Mister, don't take 'em all on yourself. Someone will slip around and shoot you in the back."

"I'm goin' to catch a nap back in those trees. If you happen to see Beckett or one of the others before I do, give me a shout or something."

"If I catch Beckett alone, there won't be nothin' left of him for you to shoot. He shouldn't have gone and beat up on Selena like that."

Andrews checked on his horses, led them deeper back into the trees, and found some fairly dry ground under a big fir tree. He unrolled his bedroll part of the way and sat on it leaning against the tree trunk. He could see the road leading into Pingree Hill, both from the east and from the west. His view of the dance hall itself was partially blocked by the trees.

The day blew clear, but the breeze was strong and cool. With his Winchester rifle across his knees, he sat perfectly still and leaned his head against the tree, flattening the back brim of his beaver felt hat.

If Beckett isn't coming back for some time, I should ride south and find Pepper. But that would leave this undone. I can't have this horse-stealin' hanging over me.

Miss Cedar, why on earth didn't you just wait at McCurleys'? You can't go runnin' around the countryside any old time you want. There's a plan to all of this, woman. I can take care of you if you follow the plan.

He tried to focus on watching the roads, but the thoughts of Suzanne Cedar riding off into the wilds of the Rocky Mountains kept nagging at him.

Tap, just forget about them wrecking the house and stealin' your horse. Go find her . . . Go find the parson. Get yourself married, boy. Don't let this blow up so close to the finish line.

Within minutes he had a dozen reasons bouncing through his mind why he should go on and find Pepper. But none of them convinced him to leave his position.

Now, Lord, this is me — Tap Andrews. I ain't prayin' for myself, mind ya. I don't got no right for that. But, Pepper, you know, Miss Cedar? Well, she's one of yours and, eh . . . well, she doesn't know this country. I mean, it sort of attracts some of the best men and some of the worst. And, well, being from the East, it will take her a while to tell the difference. So protect her and help her to do the right thing.

Staring blankly down at the road, Tap let his mind roam back to other times he had prayed. In prison . . . when Stuart Brannon had him pinned into the rocks outside of Prescott . . . when his mother died. He always figured that if there was a God, He was a long, long ways off.

But this time it felt different.

It's almost like God is listenin'. It's a little scary. That would foul things up. I surely don't need a guilty conscience over this trick I'm playin' on Miss Cedar.

Tap pulled his hat low over his eyes and leaned his head against the tree again.

I'll just close my eyes for a minute and give my mind a little rest.

It was like a distant Fourth of July celebration. Somewhere through the trees a muffled "pop," "pop" and then a cheer . . . or a shout . . . or a scream . . . or a cry.

Tap was on his feet with his Colt drawn before his eyes ever focused. He heard no more gunfire, but the screaming continued.

185

Swinging himself and his gear into the saddle, he saw several riders galloping to the east on the Fort Collins road. He reined up hard in front of the dance hall where several women were crying and in near hysterics.

"They took Selena! She's gone. They'll kill her! April's been shot. Where's a doctor? We have to have a doctor!"

Tap grabbed the sobbing girl by the shoulders and shook her. "Where's Stack? Did they kill Stack?"

"He's on the floor. It's awful bloody. He's in there!" she cried.

Dashing inside, he found the big man sprawled near the piano with a couple of girls and one short man mopping blood off his head.

"Is he shot?"

One of the women looked up. "Who are you?"

Tap kneeled down beside the man. "A friend of Stack's."

"They snuck up behind him and cold-cocked him with a carbine barrel. Then they robbed April and grabbed Selena. When they were leavin', April ran to the porch and shot at one of them. She missed, but Payton didn't."

"Payton? Was it Jordan Beckett and that bunch?" Tap asked, as he lifted the man's head.

"Oh, it was Beckett, all right. He threatened to kill every person in the building."

The big man blinked a couple of times, then opened his eyes.

"Stack? This is Tap . . . remember? We had breakfast this mornin'. Look, you're banged up, so you take care of April. I'm ridin' after them."

"You'll . . . need help . . . ," he stammered.

"I've handled them before."

"I'm goin' with you." He struggled to his feet, staggered over to a chair, and then sat down hard.

"You stay right here."

"Hatcher!" Stack hollered. "I got to go, and you know it!"

"Take care of April."

"If she's shot, I cain't do a thing for her that these girls cain't do better. Now you might not need my help, but I've got to go. I ain't of no use to April and the girls if I can't take better care of 'em, and I ain't no use to myself if I let them get the drop. I got a feelin' you understand what I'm sayin."

Tap stopped wrapping the white bandage around Stack's head and gazed at him.

"Yeah . . . you're right. You do have to come. Which is your horse?"

"I'll take the biggest one at the rail and defy any man here to protest," Stack announced, standing to his feet.

Tap mounted up. The sun was straight up, and the breeze was at their backs.

"They got us beat by fifteen minutes!" Stack hollered.

"And they probably have relays."

"We ain't goin' to catch 'em, are we?"

"Stack, they surely aren't going to Fort Collins?"

"Nope, I reckon they'll turn north and slip into Wyomin'. That's the easiest."

Suddenly Tap reined up, and Stack slid his horse to a stop alongside.

"What is it?"

"That gang is wanted up in Wyomin', right? They been comin' down here to hide."

"Yep, that's what I've heard."

"Then it doesn't make sense for them to go north."

"You figure they'll swing south?"

"Yep."

"But there's nothin' down there but a few ranches."

"Exactly. That's why we're going south. It's our only chance of catchin' 'em."

"What if we're wrong? What about Selena?"

"I don't even want to think about it. Is there a trail that swings south on down that road?"

"Well, there's a trail south at Brush Creek. I've heard that it swings around to the west and joins up with the Mineral Springs road, but I've never been on it."

"Mineral Springs?"

"Yeah, that's the road south of April's place."

"And if we cut straight south over that mountain, we should hit that trail?"

"I suppose."

"Are you feelin' like a hard ride?" Tap asked.

"I'm feelin' like makin' somebody pay."

"Let's do it!" Tap turned his pony south off the road and sprinted toward the mountains.

It was a hard hour of riding and then a hard hour of walking the horses to the top of the ridge that looked down on a thin trail by a creek below.

"That must be the Brush Creek trail." Tap pointed.

"Look down there to the west. That's where it meets the Mineral Springs road."

"Those aspen seem like a good place to set a relay team. Let's go take a look."

Riding down the grade of loose rock, they slid their way to the bottom.

"Stack, don't ride on the trail. I don't want any hoof prints to give them ideas."

"Look up there! Looks like some horse are stashed!"

Riding up the edge of the Mineral Springs road, they trotted the horses south to a small grove of aspen and found six horses in a picket line.

"These mounts are fresh. They sure haven't been here yet. You was right, Tap! They are comin' south. How did you know that?"

" 'Cause that's exactly what I would have done."

Stack pushed his hat back and scanned the horizon.

"What are we going to do now?"

"We'll cache our horses down in that draw and hike back up here. Bring that carbine and your revolver. We'll wait until they start to pull saddles off before we make a move. That way they can't ride out on us."

"But with our horses down there, we can't ride out either!" Stack cautioned.

"I wasn't plannin' on leavin' until they're all down . . . And you?" Tap quizzed.

"You're right. We ain't leavin' until we win."

Andrews stationed Stack Lowery behind some rocks between the Mineral Creek road and the aspens. Anyone who tried to make a break on horseback would face the .44 and the wrath of Lowery. Tap crouched down behind some fallen timbers near the relay horses but out of sight of the trail. He filled the last hole in the cylinder of his Colt and checked to make sure the rifle was fully loaded.

Flipping up the Vernier peep sight, he rested the gun on a log and took aim on the trail. After a few minutes he pushed the sight down and pulled the rifle behind the log.

You can only get one of them out there, and the others will scatter. We've got to fight them close range on the ground. And you have to make sure that girl doesn't get hurt worse.

Pepper's down that road someplace. She's busy makin' wedding plans and thinkin' about the future. If this backfires, she hasn't got any future. Not out West, anyway. This is crazy, Tap. You could just get on your horse, ride down there, and have the weddin' right now. Within an hour or two you could be married . . . or you could be dead.

I've got to tell her the truth. I can't keep lying. I've never lied about myself before. I'll spend my whole life trying to cover it up. Just get through this. Then ride down there and tell her. Ask her to forgive you and give you a chance to prove yourself.

Riders coming over the Brush Creek trail from the east interrupted his thoughts. He signaled Stack with his hat.

God . . . this is Tap again. I've got some things I need to take care of — important things . . . so if You bring me though this, I'll come clean with Pepper the first time I see her again.

191

The first rider was holding a gun on Selena, who was forked on the front part of his saddle, her dark dress shoved up to her knees. Following in single file were five other riders. One had a right arm in a sling, and another was bandaged on the right leg. They were the five he had faced down at the ranch. Tap didn't recognize the final rider and assumed it to be Jordan Beckett.

The breeze rolled straight at Andrews, and he figured the horses might not catch their scent. Having faced the bunch before, Tap figured he knew which ones would be the first to draw and shoot.

As they approached the aspens, the first five riders dismounted. The lead man pushed the crying girl to the ground.

"Don't hurt me no more!" she pleaded.

Get down, Beckett! Get down! She cries once more, and I know I'll move in on 'em too soon! Git off that horse!

All the men but the one with the wounded arm began to pull their saddles and toss them on the new mounts. The wounded man stood over the girl waving a revolver in his left hand.

"Jordan, you want me to finish her off now?"

"No!" The man called out.

"But there ain't no one followin' us. You said so yourself. What do we need her for?"

"We don't need her. But there's no reason

to waste a bullet and alert someone out on the road." Beckett slid out of the saddle and pulled an ivory-handled knife out of his boot.

"No!" she screamed. "No!" She tried to crawl away from the man with the gun, but he jammed his boot on her long black hair, pinning her in the mud. She began to sob hysterically.

"What's the matter, breed? I thought you liked knives!" Beckett hissed. "Wait to see what this one can do."

Just as Tap was about to raise up, the man with the wounded leg spun around and faced Beckett. "Jordan, for pete's sake, don't cut her up. Ain't no sense in that. Turn her loose. We don't need her!"

Beckett stopped and stood up as if he were considering the alternative. He let the knife drop to the ground, but as everyone's eyes followed its fall, he suddenly drew his revolver and fired two shots into the pro-testing man's chest. The others froze in place as the man dropped dead in the wet, brown grass. Even the girl stopped her sobbing and stared at the man with the smoking gun.

"Anyone else aim to tell me what I can or can't do?"

No one said anything. Andrews stood up with his rifle leveled at Beckett's head.

"Drop it, Beckett. You've shot, stole, and

kicked all the ladies you're going to for one day."

"What the . . ." Beckett stammered.

"It's that gunman from the ranch!" one of the men called out.

"Kill him!" Beckett screamed.

"Don't even think of drawin' a gun," Stack called out as he approached from the other side.

"Shoot 'em!" Beckett roared again.

"They got us from both sides," the men protested.

"We have 'em outnumbered!" Beckett screamed.

"We had 'em outnumbered at the ranch. He's crazy, Beckett. The one with the rifle is crazy!"

"You try anything, and this girl is dead," the one hovering over Selena growled. Even though his boot pinned her hair in the mud, the man yanked her head up by pulling on her hair and jammed the barrel of his revolver against her head. Andrews noticed that the single-action Colt had the hammer pulled back to the first position, but was not fully cocked.

Instantly, Tap whipped the rifle around and fired at the man threatening the girl. The bullet caught him in the upper chest, lifted him off the ground, and slammed his body at the feet of the man called Payton.

It was only seconds, but for Tap the time

seemed to stand still. The shots echoed in his ears, each one drowning out the one previous. Beckett fired two quick rounds at Stack, who dove behind the rocks. Stack's return fire caused Beckett to dive for the mud. Payton drew on Andrews but missed his shot. By then Tap had his Colt drawn and shot him in the midsection. The man stumbled back under his horse's stomach, and as he went down tried to fire another shot, but hit the horse in the leg. The terrified animal kicked the man unconscious as it limped for the Mineral Springs road.

At the same time, the man on Andrews's left leaped in panic onto his horse, but the saddle had not yet been cinched. The man crashed to the ground on the other side of the horse and met with the barrel of Stack Lowery's pistol crashing across his now hatless skull. Beckett had regained his feet and was waving a gun that was either jammed or empty.

The fifth man raised to fire his gun at Stack, but both Lowery and Andrews shot at the same time, catching him in the cross-fire.

"The knife!" Stack shouted.

Andrews dove across the sobbing Selena, rolling her toward the logs just as Beckett's knife pierced the ground where she had been. Beckett fired a shot at Lowery, who dove for cover.

Jordan Beckett sprang to his horse and began to race back east of the Brush Creek trail.

"I'll get him! You take care of Selena!" Stack called, leveling his carbine at the fleeing man.

Tap reached down and picked up Selena in his arms. She had either fainted or gotten shot. He didn't have time to determine which.

"Tap! My carbine's jammed! He's getting away!" Lowery yelled.

Tossing the girl over his left shoulder, Tap wrapped his left arm around her waist and hiked his Winchester to his chin. He lined up the peep sight on Jordan Beckett's back and waited for the rider to get at the right distance.

"Shoot him!" Stack yelled.

Tap hesitated. In the background he thought he heard a woman's voice call his name.

"Shoot him!"

"I can't, Stack . . . I've never shot a man in the back. I just can't start doin' it now."

"Mr. Hatcher!" came a high-pitched voice.

He turned to see a buggy with a horse tied behind it rolling toward them.

"What are you doing?" the woman driving the rig called out.

"Miss Pepper?" Stack called out. "I mean,

Miss Cedar! What are you doing here?"

"Pepper?" In almost a daze, Tap walked over to the buggy, still carrying his Winchester in his right hand and Selena over his left shoulder.

"What . . . who?"

"This is Rev. Houston." She nodded at the clergyman.

"What in heaven's name has happened here?" the man gasped.

"There was a robbery and a shooting, and we chased them down here."

The minister climbed out of the buggy. "A robbery? Where?"

"At April's . . . eh, at the Pingree Dance Hall," Stack offered.

"What were you doing there?" Pepper asked Tap.

"I was lookin' for my stolen horse and —"

"What stolen horse?"

"Onespot. They took him when they wrecked the ranch."

"Wrecked the ranch?"

"I went to tell you at McCurley's, but you took off."

"Took off? I came out here to get Rev. Houston lined up to do our weddin'."

"Well, Beckett and his gang shot and robbed April. Then they took —," Stack began.

"April!" Pepper gasped. "Is she —"

"That's the lady that runs the place," Tap

interrupted. "She's wounded, but I don't know how serious."

Pepper climbed out of the buggy. "Is Beckett dead?"

"No, he got away. Tap here was about to shoot him when you commenced to hollerin'," Stack explained.

"What are you doin' with her?" Pepper pointed at Selena.

"Oh . . . she's just a dance-hall girl I picked up."

Rev. Houston spun around and looked at Andrews. "You what?"

"No . . . no, not that. See, they had hauled her off as a hostage, and just now I picked her up off the ground to revive her."

"And just how did you intend to do that, Mr. Hatcher?" Pepper asked.

"Oh, I guess I can put her down." He lowered Selena off his shoulders and held her in both arms looking for a place to lay her down.

"Where should I . . . eh . . ."

Suddenly Selena blinked open her eyes and spoke softly. "I feel safe when I'm in your arms."

"She feels safe," Tap tried to explain. Suddenly he saw Selena's eyes meet Pepper's.

"You blonde witch!" she spat at Pepper and began to curse in Spanish.

"Eh . . . she must be hurt . . . don't take

any offense. She's got you confused with one of the girls down at April's," Tap stammered. Suddenly he handed Selena to Stack and glanced back at the minister who was kneeling in prayer next to one of the men.

Prayer! Oh . . . yeah . . . my promise. Lord, help me now.

"Pepper, come here." He reached out and grabbed her hesitant hand.

"What? What are you doin'? Where are we goin'?"

"Stack, take care of Selena. We'll be back in just a minute."

"Mr. Hatcher, just where are you taking me?"

"We need a private conversation. I promised God I would get this one matter cleared up right here and now. I'm not goin' to keep playin' this game," Tap insisted.

Pepper stumbled along as he pulled her back behind some trees and up an incline toward a clearing.

He knows. He knows who I am. This is it, girl. Everything he says, you deserve. You had no right to treat him this way. He merits someone a whole lot better than you.

"I know what you're going to say," she sighed. She reached up and brushed the cheeks under her eyes.

There were no tears.

"You do?"

"Certainly. It's been obvious all along."

"It has? Then why did you go along with it?" Tap asked.

"I kept hoping it would work out. Look, let me —"

"Pepper . . . just hear me out. You can ride right out of here in a minute and go back to Fort Collins, or wherever, but listen. I want you to hear this straight from me."

He took a deep breath, pulled off his hat, rolled the brim, and then looked into her green eyes.

"Pepper . . . I am not Zachariah Hatcher."

He watched her eyes grow wider and her mouth drop open.

"Hatcher and I fought off some Indians down in Arizona Territory together. He and the others died at the scene, but I lived. Before he died he —"

"You are what?" she cried.

"I am not Zachariah Hatcher. I read your letters to him . . . I was very attracted to all of this, and I tried to take his place. Now I'm tryin' to —"

"What do you mean you aren't Hatcher?" she wailed.

She's not takin' this too well. I should of beat around the bush, softened her up, laid it out subtle.

"What I'm tryin' to say is that I'm really —"

"I've been making wedding plans to marry a total stranger?" she gasped.

"Well . . . we did visit some, and I thought we were getting along, but . . . well, I'm not Hatcher. My name is Tap Andrews, and I —"

Suddenly Pepper broke out in such hysterical laughter that it completely silenced him.

8

Tap Andrews stared at Pepper's uncontrollable laughter, feeling buried by an emotional avalanche.

She's lost control. The shooting, the bodies, the dance-hall girl — it's too much for her. She shouldn't be out here. She shouldn't be saddled up with the likes of me. Maybe I better get the Reverend to look after her.

Suddenly she caught her breath and looked at him. Her expression changed to sorrow, and she began to sob.

She's lost it. She's like that Frazier woman down at Coarsegold. She went off her nut when those babies died, and she never could get it back. I kept my promise, God! I told her straight up. I need You now . . . You got to help her get control.

He had no idea what to say and absolutely no notion what to do. It was as if someone were pushing him forward as he reached out and encircled her with his arms. To his surprise, she didn't shove him away. With one hand around her waist and the other lying gently on her blonde hair that was still neatly pulled back, he held her close. He could feel the softness of her body. He could smell the sweet scent of perfume. She continued to sob.

It's our last hug. She'll ride off now. We'll wave and promise to write, but we won't. She'll go back to the East and have great adventures to share. She'll sit around some posh Chicago restaurant with her well-dressed friends, and it will all make a delightful story. "The Lady and the Gunfighter." They will laugh their way down State Street at the cowboy who thought he could marry a lady. She'll marry some banker and live in a big house, raise her kids, and sit on the porch in a rockin' chair with grandchildren runnin' around her feet. And every once in a while she'll tell 'em about the time some old cowpuncher tried to trick her, but she saw through him.

It's all I ever wanted. A ranch and a good woman. No man needs more than that. It isn't her fault. She never figured anyone would lie to her like this.

Lifting his hand from her hair, Tap smeared the tears across his cheeks and put his hand back on her golden hair.

Pepper fought to stop crying. Loosening her grip around his hard, muscled shoulders, she reached up to wipe her eyes.

There were no tears.

He's in love with Suzanne Cedar.

Thoughts of her have made this man face down that whole Beckett gang. He did it for her. He doesn't want a dance-hall girl. He's probably had all of those he wanted. Selena would fall all over him for a wink. I can't tell him now — not yet . . . Reverend, I know I promised, but . . . not now, not today, not like this. He'd leave me right there at April's. There wouldn't be nothin' left livin' for. Lord, don't You see? I know I made You some promises yesterday . . . but You've got to be patient with me. My mind wants to obey, but my heart is scared to death.

Andrews broke the silence. "Aren't you goin' to say anything?" he whispered.

"I . . . I . . . I just can't," she murmured.

He held her back at arms length but refused to look in her eyes. "Pepper, I got a favor to ask of you. I don't have any right to ask you this. But, well, would you do this for me? Would you get in that buggy and let me drive you all the way back to McCurleys'? You got to get your things anyway."

"What?" she asked.

"Just hear me out . . . please. I want you to sit in that buggy and listen to me for a while. I've got a lot of things on my heart, and if you took off to Chicago without me ever gettin' a chance to say them . . . well, I'd live with regrets all my life. Let me talk to you, please? You don't have to say a word."

He's afraid I'm goin' to leave him? Why on earth would I want to leave him?

"Just nod if you feel up to it," he insisted.

Pepper nodded.

They walked back toward the others, and he helped her into the buggy. Stack had retrieved their horses. Selena sat on a log with a blanket wrapped around her shoulders, looking sullenly at the ground. Rev. Houston had tied a bandage on one of the wounded men.

"Tap, are you feeling square? You look like you've seen the ghost of Joaquin Murietta," Stack chided.

"Well . . . it's been . . . sort of a hard time."

"Did you two clear the air?" Stack asked.

"Oh . . . that . . . you figured it out, too?"

The big man nodded.

"Reverend, what's the verdict here?" Tap questioned.

"Two dead, two will pull through, one is halfway over the edge."

"And one ran away." Stack motioned to the trail. "But he won't come back. Jordan wouldn't have the nerve to enter that dance hall without an army. Those girls would rip him to shreds before I ever got to him."

"Reverend, I'm goin' to . . . eh, drive Miss Cedar back to McCurleys'. We've got a mess of talkin' to do." Andrews stooped to retrieve several spent .44 brass cartridges as he continued the conversation.

"Yes, I know, son."

"You do? Oh, sure. I suppose everyone could see through it . . . but me. Well, I'll tie your horse with the others. Stack, I've got one of McCurley's horses tied in front of April's, and I've got papers for that black with the blaze. I'll come back for them."

"They'll be waitin'. You're stoppin' by April's, aren't you? The girls will be mighty happy to know they've been caught."

"Eh . . . no, I eh . . . well, we want to go on."

"But you're the one who stopped 'em. You ought to ride back in with the bodies."

"Stack, you can handle it here. You did your job. You brought 'em in. Go back there and take care of those ladies. If the sheriff's lookin' for me, I'll be at McCurleys' . . . or at the ranch."

Stack nodded. "I owe you one, Tap. And Stack Lowery pays his debts."

"One of these days, I'll probably have to call in that marker."

The big man reached out and shook Andrews's hand. "I'll be there. You can bank on it."

Passing by Selena, Tap glanced at her. There was mud on her face and in her hair. He noticed that she now sported two black eyes.

"Are you goin' to be all right?" he asked her.

She stood up, still holding the blanket on her shoulders. "I'll live . . . if that's what you mean."

"They didn't . . . take . . ." he stammered.

"They slapped me around and scared me with their talk, but I've gone though all that before." She glanced down. "You fell for that blonde, didn't you?"

Tap reached over and put his hand under her chin and lifted her face. Then he leaned down and kissed her gently on the lips.

"Why'd you go and do that?"

"I been wonderin' what those pretty lips taste like."

He noticed a slight twinkle in her otherwise hurting eyes. "Well?"

"Sweet . . . very sweet."

"But you're still riding off with that blonde," she pouted.

"Yep. But remember, Selena, things aren't always the way they look."

"You mean . . ."

Tap didn't look back.

"Reverend, I suppose you know it already, too, but we won't be needin' your services right away. In fact, I don't rightly know if we'll need 'em at all."

"Yes, yes, I understand. I had a long conversation with Pepper yesterday," the minister acknowledged.

"Well, maybe someday we can sit down, and I'll try to explain it all to you," Tap offered.

"I'll look forward to it," the clergyman said nodding.

Tap tipped his hat to Stack and hiked up the hill to the buggy. Tying his horse to the back of the buggy, he climbed in and slapped the lines against the drive horse's rump. They rolled out of sight of the others before either spoke a word.

"Do you often kiss women like that?"

"You mean dance-hall girls? Well —"

"No, I meant so tenderly. Why did you kiss that girl on the lips?" Pepper asked.

" 'Cause she's been beat up real bad the past couple of days. I expect she's feelin' poorly on the outside and even worse inside. She just looked like she needed someone to treat her gentle."

"And it's your job to see that all women are happy?"

"No, ma'am, but my heart hurts when I see women and children treated poorly. If she'd been five years old, I probably would have done the same thing."

"On the lips?"

Tap could feel himself blush. "Well, maybe not on the lips."

"Are you going to stop at the dance hall?"

"Nope. Now I need to tell you some things

that have been bustin' to get out for days."

When they reached the Fort Collins road, he turned the rig west, and neither looked back at Pingree Hill. The sun had started on its downward journey and would be in their eyes for the next several hours. Although the day was clear, a cool breeze blew directly into their faces. Tap pulled his hat down in the front, and Pepper wrapped herself in a blanket.

"Pepper, I'm going to do a lot of talkin'. And I probably won't come up for air too often. Now I don't mean to be impolite, but there are things you need to hear.

"I believe in bein' real honest, and that's why this thing about pretendin' to be Hatcher was eatin' me to death. Now the truth is, well . . . I'm hopin' that I can tell you somethin' that would cause you to want to stay out here in Colorado and give me a chance to prove myself as worthy a man as Mr. Zachariah Hatcher. Now . . . I mean, I know I can't be as worthy as him in your sight, but maybe I could . . . you know . . . be acceptable.

"Say, are you gettin' cold? I'll stop and build a fire and heat some rocks if you'd like," he offered.

"No, no, please continue," Pepper urged.

"Well . . . let me tell you who I really am. I was born along the Tuolumne Creek in California."

"I didn't know anyone was born in California."

"Well, my daddy was a prospector. He still is a prospector . . . I think."

"Where is he?"

"His name's Anson Andrews, and he went to Australia to hunt for gold in '72, and I haven't heard from him since. Anyway, my mama was a métis. Are you familiar with the term?"

"Only slightly."

"Well, she was born up in the British possessions of a French father and an Indian mother. Anyway, she died when me and Stoddard were still pretty young. I can barely remember her."

"Stoddard?"

"My younger brother, Stoddard."

"Your name is Tapadera, and your brother is Stoddard?"

"Yeah, Mama named me, and Daddy named my brother. We're about as different as our names."

"Where's your brother now?"

"Most of him is buried at Fort Lincoln, I think."

"Most of him?"

"He was with General Crook at the Battle on the Rosebud. He served with Captain Noyes, 2nd Cavalry, D Troop. I was told he got hacked up pretty bad."

"What about other family?"

"You mean grandparents, uncles, cousins?"

"Yes."

"Well, as far as I know, I don't have any. Sounds lonely, doesn't it?"

Pepper nodded.

"Are you gettin' hungry? I might have a little supper left from the McCurleys down in my saddlebags. We can stop and check on it."

"No, no, please continue."

"Well, one of my father's friends settled into the store business in Sacramento, so me and my brother were left there to get our schooling and all. We stayed with those folks until, well, Stoddard stayed there until he joined the army."

Pepper shaded her eyes and looked over at Tap. "When did you leave home?"

"I never figured I really had a home, but I left those folks when I was fifteen. Things were just beginnin' to open up in the Comstock, and I hiked over the Sierras to 'see the elephant.' "

"Did you work in the mines?" she pressed.

"Only for a little while. I found out I get real nervous down in those shafts, so I worked up on top, helpin' around at the . . . eh, I was always . . . anyway, I got by. But as soon as I saved up a little, I went down to New Mexico and hired on with old John

211

Chisum out along the Pecos."

"So you're a cowboy?"

"Well, I did my share of ropin' and brandin' over the years. But sometimes I'd hire on to ride guard for the stage line, or to make sure things didn't get out of hand at a gamblin' house, or to see that Indians didn't attack a survey party . . . and stuff like that."

"You mean, you're a hired gun?"

"Straight up, I guess you could call me that."

"No wonder you took on all of Beckett's gang."

"Well, that was a little foolhardy. I just figured you and the ranch were worth fightin' for."

"So you bounced around New Mexico with your gun for sale?" she asked.

"West Texas, New Mexico, Arizona. I even served as a deputy marshal in San Bernardino, California, for a few months."

"And you probably know every dance-hall girl in three states."

He looked over at her to see if she was angry, serious, or joking. Her green eyes revealed nothing.

"But how did you meet Zachariah Hatcher?" she asked.

"Eh . . . that's gettin' ahead of things a bit. First, I've got to tell you about prison," Tap admitted.

"You served time in prison!" she gasped.

"Well, not a whole lot, but . . . well, it's a long story. Last year I was workin' as shipment guard on a run between Tucson and Globe City. Well, there was this lady —"

"Somehow I knew a woman was in this," Pepper interrupted.

"Miss Cedar, I promised I'd tell you the truth. Now I'd just as soon skip this part if you want me to. I ain't necessarily proud of it none."

"No, no, go on."

"Well, me and this lady in Globe City was being real chummy. Ever' time I'd come into town, we'd do some . . . eh, visitin'.'"

"I can imagine."

"Well, one night we were sittin' in a room at the International Hotel in Globe City where we were . . . eh, well . . .'"

"Visitin'?"

"Right. We were visitin' real friendly like, and a red-faced man waving a gun burst into the room claiming to be the woman's husband. Now, Miss Pepper, it's the honest truth, I didn't know this lady was married at all. Well, he's rantin' and ravin' and threatenin' to shoot me, when all of a sudden this raven-haired woman pulls my revolver off the night table and shoots him dead with one shot."

"Her own husband?"

"Yep. Well, as you can imagine, quite a ruckus broke out. She's a sobbin' and cryin' over the man she just murdered, and all I want to do is get out of there. So I leave her to explain how she killed him, and I jump on my pony and ride north."

"And she told them you killed her husband?"

"Well, not directly, no. They just jumped to that conclusion and wouldn't listen to her confession. The next thing I know, most of Arizona is chasin' after me, includin' Stuart Brannon himself."

"Brannon — the one in all those dime novels?"

"That's the one."

"There really is such a man?"

"Oh, yeah. He's for real. They cornered me up in some rocks in Yavapai County — Brannon and four or five others. I told Brannon what really happened, and he promised me a trial, so I gave up."

"What happened at the trial? Did the wife back up your story?"

"Well, it seems she disappeared, and no one knew where she was. They put out papers to have her arrested, but I can't stand to think about any woman goin' to jail, so I didn't tell them what really happened."

"And they convicted you?"

"Yep. Crime of passion, they called it.

Gave me ten years at A.T.P. in Yuma."

"How long were you there?"

"Six months. Then I escaped."

"How did you get out?"

"Uh . . . well, the warden's wife sort of helped me. She's a good woman."

"Did you kiss her gently to make her feel better when you left?" Pepper quizzed.

"What? Oh . . . no, no . . . nothin' like that. But she did lend me sixty cash dollars."

"Why sixty?"

" 'Cause they were offerin' fifty dollars to any Mojave Indian who brought an escaped prisoner back to A.T.P. So when I got caught, I offered him sixty dollars to let me go."

"When was this?"

"About a month, six weeks ago. You see, I made my way up to northern Arizona and hopped a stage to Utah. But before it got too far, we were chased by a bunch of Navajo warriors. It seems they were out to get revenge on whites who had killed an Indian family that week. Well, we were the lucky ones that ended up being the target."

"And Zachariah Hatcher was on that stage?"

"Yes, ma'am, he was."

"As it turned out, all of 'em got killed but me. Your Mr. Hatcher was the last to go, and I took care of him most of the night.

That's when I learned about the letters, the ranch, and how you two had never met, and all that."

"So then you decided to be Mr. Hatcher?"

"Well, I had promised him to come up here and tell you what happened. But when I get to Mexican Wells, one of the girls there thought I actually was Hatcher. So it gave me the idea to try this scheme. Listen, Miss Cedar, I read those letters you wrote to him so many times, I . . . I felt like I knew you. Hatcher had everythin' goin' for him, and then one lousy day ends the whole thing. Me, I figure most of my life's been pretty shallow and empty, so maybe it was my turn to have a break. I just was hopin' maybe we'd hit it off, and I'd tell you later."

"Like when they came to arrest you for escaping from prison?"

"Well, I kind of hoped I could put that part in the past. Arizona officials won't come up here. Someday I'll find Rena, and she'll —"

"Rena?"

"That raven-haired lady. Her name was Rena. I don't guess I'll ever forget the way she could —"

"I think I'll skip this part," Pepper interrupted.

"Yeah . . . well, if I find her, I figure she'll clear this thing up. And . . . well, you know all the rest from there."

Pepper sat still for a long time.

"Miss Cedar . . . that's all in the past. I'd like a chance to be different. I've been square with you, and you know more about Tap Andrews than any other living soul. Seems like I've lived for years without ever talkin' personal with anyone."

The sun went down, but they continued to ride into the night. She sat closer to Tap and pulled the blanket to cover both of their laps.

"Maybe it's time for a fire and warming some foot rocks," she suggested.

He pulled off the road, rested the driving horse, and built a fire. Eating the few leftovers he had in his saddlebags, they hovered over the small fire and gazed at each other across the flickering flames. He had the top button on his coat fastened down and the rest left open. As always, the handle of his Colt was in plain sight . . . and touch. Pepper used the blanket as a shawl on top of her cape. A good portion of her hair had jostled free from the confinement of her hat, and it tousled to her shoulders.

"Well, Mr. Tapadera Andrews," she sighed. "Where do we go from here?"

"You mean, you and me?"

"Yes. Where does all this leave us?"

"I figured you would ask that. But, of course, I can only tell you my opinion.

217

These rocks are pretty warm. Are you ready to continue?"

"You won't forget this conversation, will you?" she pressed.

"Nope. You can count on it."

Andrews used one of the blankets to protect his hands and lifted the big round stones to the carriage, placing them in the metal warming box that served as a footboard.

By the time they boarded, Pepper could feel the heat rise from the box, warming her feet, legs, and even the blanket in her lap. "Now, Mr. Andrews, you were saying —"

"You really can call me Tap."

"Now that just might depend on what you say next, doesn't it?"

"Eh . . . yeah, I guess it does. Well, I'm going to ask you a favor that I don't have any right to ask. First, I'd like to go back and put you in the McCurley Hotel. I'd plan on stayin' out at your ranch."

"My ranch? What do you mean my ranch?" Pepper questioned.

"Hatcher told me to bring you the papers for the ranch. He truly wanted you to have it. He said you could sell it or do anything you wanted, but it was yours. I'll give you the deed when we get to the hotel."

"But I can't . . . I don't know —"

"Just let me continue with my dream."

"Dream?"

"Yeah, a dream is something you want to have happen real bad, but you don't figure it ever will. As I said, you stay at the hotel, and me at the ranch. I'll develop the property and start a little cow and calf operation for you. In the meantime, we have an opportunity to get to know each other. Then . . . you know, if things work out . . . well, maybe we could . . . you know . . . send for the parson after all. Now I know I'm not Hatcher. But Hatcher is gone to his reward. You know, it was the strangest thing. I almost forgot it."

"What?"

"When your man died, he was talkin' about you. All of a sudden I can remember his words. He said, 'Tell her I loved her, Andrews. Tell her I loved her more than anything in this whole world. The Lord will take care of her' and then . . ."

"Then?"

"Well, he was sufferin' mighty fierce, his face in terrible pain. Then there was this big smile like he saw somethin' or someone. I looked out in the desert, but I couldn't see anythin'. Then he died. I didn't know if he was seein' you or Jesus. I never did see a person go like that. Did you?"

"Only once." Pepper reached up with her gloved hand and brushed her tearless cheeks.

"As I was sayin', I'm not competing

against Hatcher. If he was here, I wouldn't be interferin' at all."

"You wouldn't?"

Andrews paused for a long while.

"I promised to be honest with you, didn't I?"

"Straight up, you said."

"Okay, if Hatcher was here, I'd probably try somethin' to steal you away, but the point is — he's not here, and both your life and my life need to go on."

If it had been daylight and if he had been looking at her, he could have seen a wide smile roll across her face.

"And what if, after this trial period, we find each other wretched?" she asked.

"Then I promise to ride off and not hassle you further."

"Would this be like an engagement?"

"I hadn't thought about that . . . I mean, if you're willin'. Would you really want to be engaged to me?" he pursued.

"Perhaps. If that is what it will take to keep you from kissing dance-hall girls on the lips."

"Miss Cedar, you can bank on that. If we're really engaged, well . . . I'll never kiss another dance-hall girl again!"

"That's a promise," she laughed, "that neither you nor I expect you to keep. But, please, I like it better when you call me Pepper."

"Well, now I heard that depends on how this conversation is goin'. How is it goin'?"

"Very good," she added quickly, "as far as we've gone, that is."

"You mean we've got more to talk about?"

"You've been doing all the talking," she reminded him.

Tap switched the reins from the left to his right hand. He stretched his left arm behind him in the buggy and thought for a moment about placing it around her shoulders. Then he hesitated.

"Look," she blurted out, "are you going to put that arm around me or not?"

"Oh . . . well, I . . ." He slid his arm around her and pulled her just a little closer to himself.

"Tap Andrews, I need to tell you lots and lots of things. But I need to ask you one question first."

"I hope I can answer it."

"So do I. Mr. Hatcher was very clear about his Christian faith in his letters. It was certainly one of his strengths. I've not heard you mention the Lord's place in your life."

He immediately pulled his arm from her shoulder and replaced in on the reins in front of him.

"Did I say something wrong?"

"No, miss . . . eh, Pepper. I just need a chance to gather my thoughts."

The night was moonless, but the stars

were bright, and a faint reflection on the road could be seen except when they passed through some trees. Pepper felt safe, fairly warm, and slightly nervous.

I don't want to lose him. I like being with this man. He makes me smile . . . he makes me cry . . . he makes me like being me. He makes me talk better, act better, think better. Tap Andrews, why wasn't it you that carried me off when I was fifteen?

Lord, this is Pepper. You know, when I prayed with the Reverend yesterday, I meant what I said about Jesus. You are Lord now. But . . . well, I just can't tell him I ain't her. Not yet. Give me just a little more time.

Pepper didn't press him to answer the question.

Tap's mind flashed to one answer after another.

I could try to fake it and pretend to be spiritual like Hatcher. But she'd see right through that and never trust me again. I can play it by ear — just say what she wants me to hear . . . I could . . . I could just straight out tell her the truth.

"I'll make you a promise, Pepper. I've lied to you for the last time. You can like my answer or hate it. But it will be true. I'm not perfect in a lot of ways . . . but I'm honest, and here's the square talk about my faith."

He cleared his throat and looked straight

ahead into the darkness. Even though the night air was cool, he could feel sweat forming on his forehead.

"Pepper, if you would have asked me that question a month ago, I would have had an easy answer. Over the years, me and God mostly ignored each other. I didn't have any Christian upbringin', and I didn't exactly hang around with a church crowd, if you catch which way the stick's floatin'. I haven't bothered Him much, and He hasn't bothered me. But it started with Hatcher's death, like I told ya . . . well, I've been givin' it more thought than ever before.

"For a long time I was pretty disappointed with God. I guess it's because I pled with Him when my mother was so sick, and she died anyway. That's when I felt all alone in the world, and basically I've been all alone ever since.

"But after I watched Hatcher die, I started thinkin' about prayin'. For the life of me, I have no idea why after all these years, I decided I needed to pray. I think it was because I could feel the charade slipping away and wanted it to work more than anythin' in the world. So back there in the trees I prayed that if I could pull through that scrape, I'd tell you the truth.

"I feel like there just might be somethin' to this faith stuff, 'cause I've never felt God really cared, and now I'm beginnin' to think

He's not so far away as I thought. Maybe that isn't a good answer. It's not the answer you wanted, but it's true, and I'm hopin' you'll give me time to learn some more. I've got a whole bunch to learn, but I know you'll be a good teacher."

Me? He wants me to teach him about the Lord! This is too new! Look, I'm just a dance-hall girl who barely started believin' . . . I can't . . .

"Miss Pepper, are you awake?" he finally asked.

"Oh . . . yes . . . I'm terribly sorry . . . It's been quite a long night."

"Well, I'm counting on you teachin' me out of the Bible. I want to learn some more."

"Perhaps you should ask the Reverend to come by. I'm sure he could answer your questions better than I could. He mentioned coming back out here before Christmas."

Both of them were real quiet for the longest time. The sunlight and slight wind during the day had dried the road enough that it no longer threw mud. They bounced softly down the road with the only noise the clomp of the horses hooves and the occasional squeak of a buggy wheel.

Suddenly Tap sat up and blurted out, "Before Christmas!"

Pepper, who had been dozing on his shoulder, jumped and gasped.

"Oh . . . sorry," he apologized. "You were asleep, weren't you?"

"What did you say . . . about Christmas?" she asked.

"You said the Reverend would be over before Christmas, and I could talk with him then."

"Yes, of course . . ."

"That means you're not goin' back to Chicago until after Christmas! You're willin' to give it a try?"

"I think your plan sounds good. We should give it some time," she added.

"Are we engaged then?" he asked.

"You haven't asked me to marry you. How can we be engaged?" she responded.

Tap Andrews immediately pulled the buggy to the side of the road and reached over and took her gloved hands into his gloved hands. Even though it was still dark, he looked into her eyes. "Miss Suzanne Cedar, what with your father being deceased and all, I'm asking you directly — will you marry me? Eh . . . providin' we end up . . . you know . . . likin' each other?"

With her left hand still in his, she removed her right hand and brushed her eyes.

There were no tears.

"Tap . . . my heart says yes. But I'm not sayin' yes because it wouldn't be fair."

"What do you mean — fair?"

"Well, you asked me to marry you, and you haven't spent a night listenin' to my story yet. I don't think you should ask until you've heard from me first."

"Are you tellin' me that Miss Suzanne Cedar has some hidden secrets?"

"Perhaps."

"I can't imagine anythin' you could tell me that would make me change my mind."

Pepper sighed and squeezed his hands. "I can."

"Let me get this straight. If after I hear all those hidden secrets, if I still want to marry you, you promise to say yes?"

"Don't forget you promised to visit with Rev. Houston . . . and we'll need to end up likin' each other."

"I can't believe it!" Tap sighed. "I don't think I ever felt this good in my whole life!"

"But you haven't heard me out," she cautioned.

"Pepper, I don't care . . . things are takin' a turn. I can feel a real swing for the better. Can you feel it? It's just like in a gun battle when you know you're goin' to win!"

He glanced over at her and thought he could see her smile.

"Now, listen. I haven't spent much time around Eastern ladies, and if I get improper, you tell me straight out to stop it, and I will. You promise?"

"Just what do you intend to do?"

She saw his right hand reach over. She felt the strong, callused, yet tender fingers lift her chin. Her heart jumped when she felt his warm lips press gently against hers.

Suddenly, he sat back up and slapped the reins, bringing the buggy back to the road.

The evening sky was starting to turn to daylight by the time they came to the flat stretch just a few miles from McCurley's hotel. He knew she had been dozing in and out of sleep for a couple hours, but, without looking down, he could sense her eyes were open.

"What are you thinkin' about?" he asked.

"If I ever, ever catch you kissin' another woman like you did that dark-haired . . . well, I'll . . . I'll rip her lips out with my own hands!" She giggled.

"Now you're talkin', Pepper! You been out here long enough to get into the gallop of things. Why, you almost sounded just like one of these dance-hall girls yourself."

Immediately she stopped giggling.

9

Pepper climbed the stairs to her room at the McCurley Hotel with her eyes barely open. Totally exhausted, she figured she could have lain down in the middle of the road and fallen asleep. Her last words before entering the hotel were a sleepy promise to have a very long talk with Tap as soon as they both rested up.

I can't tell him now. I'm so tired . . . I wouldn't explain it right. Just a little rest. He's so . . . so tough . . . and yet tender. I saw his tears. What will he do when he learns that the proper Eastern lady that he dreams about died in my arms? Will he rant, or will he weep . . . or will he do both?

Pepper pulled off her dress and laid it carefully over a Queen Anne green velvet chair. Her heavy eyelids stayed open long enough for her to brush down the dress. Sitting on a stool at the foot of the bed, she unlaced her black boots, tugged them off, and removed her stockings. Wiggling her toes, she went to the window and drew the white lace curtains closed. Then she folded back the comforter on her bed and crawled between the covers.

Looking back, she didn't even remember laying her head on the pillow.

No worry about hidden secrets.

No planning a wedding.

No dreams about a dark-haired, brown-eyed man.

Just sleep.

"Pepper? Pepper, dear? Are you feeling well?"

The room was dark. Too dark.

She sat up in the bed and pulled a flannel sheet around her.

"What? What is it?"

It was Mrs. McCurley's voice filtering through the door. "Pepper . . . will you be taking supper downstairs?"

"Supper? Is it that late?"

"You were very tired."

"I'll be down. Can I have a few minutes?"

"Certainly. The others are eating now, but there will be plenty."

After a few hurried moments of dressing, she stood at the mirror combing her hair.

Maybe I should leave it down when I talk to him? It's more . . . informal. Or . . . maybe I should just reach up and let it tumble down right before I begin to explain. Yes, that would be much more theatrical.

No . . . not that. You're right, Lord. He told it to me straight, and I'll do the same with him. But it's harder for me. He's always been one to tell the truth. I've spent my whole life lyin' to myself and to the men. Lord, it's not easy talkin' about the truth 'cause there isn't very much that's true about me that I like. I'm better at lyin' than truthin'.

With her hair pinned back and her dress in place, Pepper descended the stairs and entered the dining room. The men stood to their feet as she entered, and she nodded to signal them to be reseated.

"Is someone leaving?" she asked Mrs. McCurley after she was sitting down. "I noticed the trunks in the hallway."

"Those are yours. They came over on the stage today, but I didn't want to wake you up."

"Mine?"

"Yes. From Fort Collins . . . and some mail."

"Oh . . . well . . . so soon? I hardly wrote."

"I guess when the stage delivered your letter, they were happy to get the trunks out of their way and sent them back on the same stage. Robert will help you get them up to your room after supper."

Pepper glanced around at the guests in the dining room.

"Are you looking for Mr. Andrews?"

"Andrews?" Pepper sounded startled. "He told you about himself?"

"Oh, yes, he explained the whole thing to

Mr. McCurley and myself. You know, Robert wasn't a bit surprised. Said he knew Tap didn't handle those guns like an ordinary drover. One thing I can tell you . . ."

She leaned over and spoke in hushed tones. "He certainly is taken with you! Why, he carried on and on like a schoolboy. You wouldn't think such a . . . a tough man would say such . . . well, such sweet things, would you?"

"He's full of contrasts, isn't he?" Pepper smiled.

"Yes . . . that's it. Now I don't think that stunt of pretending to be Hatcher was very honest, but it was terribly romantic. He said he fell in love with you reading the letters. Can you imagine that? Oh . . . I'm sure you can imagine it."

"Yes . . . it has been a very interesting relationship. Mrs. McCurley, I don't see Tap. Has he already eaten?"

"Oh, my, he went back to the ranch hours ago. Why, he didn't even stay until noon."

"He didn't?"

"He said he was so excited he couldn't rest. He wanted to go clean up the house. I hear they made a horrid mess."

"He's really . . . not . . . not here?" Pepper stammered.

"After telling us his story, he bought some groceries and some boards, borrowed our buckboard and Mr. McCurley's carpentry tools, and scooted off to the ranch. He is very intent on gettin' it all fixed up for you. I'd say you got yourself a real worker. My Robert — he's a real worker, too. Honey, there's nothin' on earth worse than a lazy husband. Take my sister, Sarah, for instance. Well, she up and married —"

"But . . . we needed . . . I mean, I wanted —"

"You know, dear, you do look pale," Mrs. McCurley observed. "Have some more boiled potatoes and gravy. Did I tell you that's an elk roast? The gravy is superb, if I do say so myself."

"When is he coming back?"

"Mr. Andrews? Why, I don't know that I heard. Robert? Robert, did Tap say when he was coming back?"

Bob McCurley looked up at his wife with a bite of roast the size of a small apple speared on his knife. "Tap? Oh, he'll be back when he gets those repairs made, I reckon. Evenin', Miss Cedar."

"Evenin', Mr. McCurley."

"He was worried about all you went through. Figured you needed plenty of rest. Why, he told us all about the shootout. My, that does sound frightenin'. He was mighty proud of you that you didn't faint. Most ladies from the East would have outright fainted."

"Actually, by the time I got there, most

of the shootin' was over," Pepper explained.

"Oh, yes . . . he said he had the girl in the blue dress over his shoulder when you drove up."

"He told you that?"

"Well . . . yes. He also mentioned how upset you got when he kissed that poor hurt dance-hall girl."

"What? I can't believe he told you all this!"

"Like I said, my Robert and I think Mr. Andrews is a very fine fellow. We certainly wish you two the best. Frankly," she whispered, "having a man like that is almost like having a sheriff in the area. If you catch the drift."

"Did he tell you what happened in the buggy on the way home?" Pepper asked.

"Ah!" Mrs. McCurley put her hand to her mouth. "No! What happened?"

"Oh, nothing!" Pepper beamed.

At least he knows how to keep some things private.

After supper she supervised as Bob McCurley and another man hefted two trunks to her room. She carried in her hand two letters.

After she was alone, Pepper stared at the trunks.

"Now, Lord, I'm going to send all this stuff right back to her mother, but . . . well, I don't have any address to send them to. So as soon as I find that little coin purse with the keys . . ."

She began to dig through her own belongings in a dresser drawer. "I'll peek inside long enough to know where to return them. I'll have to write a letter explaining her death . . . oh, I wish I'd had Rev. Houston write a letter!"

Both trunks were filled with neatly packed personal items. Dresses, shoes, hats, gloves, undergarments, books, pencils, stationery, several photographs, a sewing box, and jewelry. She sorted each trunk slowly, holding every item up to her in the mirror and trying to imagine how it would be to wear.

Now this would look lovely at a party. I wonder if they have parties out here? Sure . . . we can have a party at the ranch and invite the McCurleys and . . . well, there has to be other people around here.

I'd wear the yellow to church, and perhaps I could make Tap a . . . but we don't have a church. Well . . . I'll just wear them every day. That ought to keep him comin' in early.

And this . . . oh, my . . . is this the way it goes? Well, I'm goin' to wear it anyway. Providin' the shutters is all drawn.

Suzanne Cedar, I'm not playin' with your valuables . . . they're just so pretty. This is more clothing than I've ever owned in my

234

whole life. She dabbed a little perfume on her wrists and smelled it.

"Suzanne, girl, I'm glad you aren't around. You would be hard to compete with. This stuff would attract every man for thirty miles!"

But neither trunk contained any address of Miss Cedar's mother or any other relative. Having folded and repacked everything, she closed and locked the lids.

After an all-day sleep, Pepper didn't feel tired, but she slipped into her flannel gown and carried the lantern to the bedstand. She set Suzanne Cedar's Bible down on the bed and retrieved the two letters. Climbing up on the comforter, she sat cross-legged and stared at them.

Finally she spoke aloud, "Suzanne, look, I can't send your trunks back, or your mail, or your money until I have an address. So I'm going to open these letters to find out where all of this goes."

She slowly unfolded the heavy parchment letter and held it over to the light to read it better.

Dearest Suzanne,

Honey, I hated so much to see you leave for fear I would never see you again. We must all release our loved ones into God's care, but I have had such a struggle since your father's death that I selfishly wanted you to remain, although the quarters here, as you know, are quite cramped.

I didn't want to tell you while you were here that I have had a real heaviness of heart and pains in my chest of late. I will see a doctor tomorrow and write to you about it.

I am thrilled with your Mr. Hatcher. He is a very fortunate man to steal your affections as he has. Darling, I'm sure you're doing the right thing! If I were your age, I would hope to have the nerve to do the same. I would like to think there'll be a day I can come west and meet him, but I have serious doubts that such a day will arrive.

With your father gone, I feel so empty inside. I'm not sure he ever knew how my every thought was on him. I hope you will feel that way someday about your Mr. Hatcher. The love was so sweet that it well compensates for the sorrow I now feel.

Write to me as soon as you get settled.

With much love,
Mother.

Write soon to where? Where's the address? You don't write a letter and not put on the address.

Obviously Suzanne knew the address.

She picked up the other letter and immediately recognized that it was different handwriting.

Suzanne, child,

I'm sorry to have to tell you such sad news, but your mama died last Monday. The doctor said it was a heart attack, but I do believe it was a combination of losing your father and then you running off and breaking her heart.

Young people seem so bent on going their own ways. We did not think it proper to wait for your return, so we had her buried here in Chicago. Doctors and burying is expensive here, but don't worry, your mother's savings covered it. I'll store her things in the attic, but I don't expect you'll want to come back now.

Sincerely,
Aunt Pearl

She died! Just like that? Dead . . . buried . . . gone? No address? Lord, there's no address! What do I do now?

Pepper laid back on the pillow and picked

up Suzanne Cedar's Bible. She flipped it open to the New Testament and began to read the verses that had been underlined.

It was well after midnight, and she was on her second lantern when she finished reading some verses in the last two chapters of Revelation — and a note Suzanne had scrawled on the bottom of the page: "Lord, help me keep at least one sinner from facing Your just wrath."

"Well, Suzanne girl, you just might have got that prayer answered."

She rested the open Bible on her chest and closed her eyes. Then suddenly she sat straight up.

"That's what I'll do!"

Jumping out of bed, she opened one of the trunks and removed several sheets of paper and two pencils. Then she began a careful inventory of every item in each trunk, describing them in detail. When she completed this, she counted and stacked the inheritance money on the dresser and any other personal effects of Suzanne Cedar's.

It was two hours later when she completed the list and inserted it in the Bible. She turned out the flickering light and crawled underneath the covers. Then she quickly slid out of bed, grabbed up the Bible, and in the dark knelt beside it.

Lord, it's me . . . Pepper. I'm not botherin'

You, am I? I could talk to You in the mornin'
if you want, but I couldn't figure any way
to return these things that belong to Miss
Cedar. So I've made a list, and if You bring
someone along that lays claim to them, I'll
return every last item and every last penny,
no matter how many years I need to work.
But in the meantime, I'm goin' to use them
like they were . . . sort of, loaned to me from
You. I won't sin with them, and I'll try to do
the kinds of things Miss Cedar would.
Thank You, and good-bye. I mean, in Jesus'
name, amen. Oh . . . yeah . . . I'm goin' to
tell Tap the very next time I see him, I
promise.

For over an hour she practiced each line
she would use to tell him that she was not
really Suzanne Cedar. She finally fell
asleep, thinking of strong arms and a gentle
kiss.

Tap was halfway back to the ranch before
he realized how tired he was. In the buckboard he had packed supplies to rebuild
the ranch house and resupply the pantry.
Brownie was tied behind the wagon.

"Tap, old boy, she's goin' to give you a
chance to prove you can live up to Hatcher's
standards! Now that's the first decent break
you've had in years.

"I'll fix up that place real nice . . . why,
she could even invite her Eastern friends

to come out and spend some time with us. Yes, ma'am, it will be a first-rate ranch. 'Course, we may go broke, but it will be first-rate broke!

"Why, I'm mighty pleased to meet you, Mr. Eastern Banker! And this must be your lovely wife. Well, Pepper . . . I mean, Suzanne has told me such delightful stories of you two!

"Excuse me? Oh . . . you're the professor from the university? Well, yes, we could ride up to the ridge for some geological studies, I suppose. Of course, I'm only a rank amateur.

"Well, you don't say. You sing on the stage in New York? No, no . . . I've never been there. You must have me confused with some other man. Why, thank you, ma'am . . . and you look right handsome yourself.

"Now, Pepper, we were just visitin'. After all, these are *your* friends."

The sun warmed him all over after he turned northeast on the trail. He dozed as the team of horses plodded down the grade to the mouth of the canyon. Long shadows of late afternoon spread before him when the ranch house came into view. Several longhorn cattle grazed near the house.

"Well, you all moseyed down to the barn, did you? Now look at that — old daddy stayed out of the bog and came looking for the wives and kids, did he?"

The brown and white bull took one look at the oncoming wagon, let out a bellow and a snort, and then circled behind the house, trotting back up the valley. Soon the entire little herd followed.

By the time Andrews drew up to the house, the only animal in sight was the gray and white cat sprawled on top of the roof, soaking up the last rays of declining sunlight.

Tap unloaded the supplies on the porch and took the team to the barn, turning them and Brownie out for the night.

Andrews spent the next several hours making as many repairs as he could. Finding a glass pane in the attic, he repaired the bedroom window. Then he patched up the dining table and several chairs and completely scrubbed the kitchen. He didn't have leathers to retie the bed, but he built it with rough-sawn boards instead.

I'll find us some real bed springs — that's what I'll do. Bob McCurley has them at the hotel. There must be some more somewhere. This room needs a picture! And maybe some paneling . . . and a wardrobe. Where does a woman put her dresses? You don't just hang 'em on a peg, do ya?

It was midnight when he stretched out his bedroll on the wood frame bed. Using an extra blanket, he propped up his head and turned up the lantern. Then he pulled out Zachariah Hatcher's Bible.

She wants a Christian husband. Now that's a reasonable request. But I'm not sure what that means. I won't get drunk. I won't gamble our money away. I won't go to chasin' dance-hall girls, and I won't lay a hand on her to harm her. I'll go to church . . . if we ever have one close, and I'll read the Bible. I guess I could learn to say grace at the table, but . . . well, I reckon there must be more to it than that!

He started to read something called "The Preface to the King James Version," but got bogged down, so he went to the table of contents.

Look at this? I can't pronounce half of these words! And these are just the titles of the books. Deut-teron-ronomy. Ec-Eccles-si . . ." Oh, forget that one. *"Mal-malac-hi. John. John?"*

That sounds more like it. Page 1024. 1024 pages! It will take me twenty years to read this! Pepper, you aren't goin' to make me read the whole thing first, are you?

Here it is . . . "The Gospel According to Saint John." Let's see . . . "In the beginning was the Word, and the Word was with God, and the Word was God. . . ."

Andrews figured he'd fall asleep by the time he'd read a couple pages. That's why he was surprised, two hours later, when he

242

finished the last chapter of John. He laid the Bible down, turned off the lantern, and scrunched around on the hard bed boards. Every bone in his body ached from the activities of the past several days. He could feel the tension of his mind begin to recede.

I'm not sure where this is leadin', but it's beginnin' to feel like I'm on the right trail.

About 3:30 in the morning Tap finally fell asleep.

The bright sun cast short shadows when the gray and white cat pounced on his chest. He jumped out of bed, grabbed his Colt, and searched for phantoms.

It proved to be a mild Indian summer day as Andrews finished cleaning up the strewn debris in the yard. In late afternoon he saddled up Brownie and rode to the treeless hills that bordered the ranch to the west. Leaving the horse tied to a boulder, he hiked further up the exposed granite until, panting and soaked with sweat, he reached the summit of the ridge.

Straining to see to the south, he could follow the North Platte to where the Canadian and the Michigan Rivers forked.

"Well, somewhere down there is McCurley's hotel."

He wiped the sweat on his shirt sleeve and glanced to the southeast at the Rocky Mountains. "They are big . . . so very big!

Sort of reminds me how puny people are. God, I sure don't know how You can look down here and ever spot us at all. It would take a whole lot more than a long-range peep sight."

He studied the horizon as he remembered what he had read the night before. For over an hour he recalled different events in his life. Some brought smiles. Some drew tears. And some caused him to blush with shame.

Finally, he took a deep breath and stood up, pacing among the rocks at the crest of the butte.

"Now, God . . . I know I'm supposed to do somethin' right now. But I . . . I just, well, I . . . I'm just not too sure what to do. But I'll tell You somethin' — that part I read last night about You bein' the way. Well . . . I believe it! I don't know why I believe it, but just readin' it last night and thinkin' about it now on this mountain, I know it's true. I believe You're big enough to forgive me, and You know I need forgivin' as much as anybody on this earth ever needed forgivin'.

"Now, Jesus, You might not have expected to land such a worthless fish, but You got me hooked good. And, eh . . . I don't back away once I make up my mind.

"I'm hopin' that this sits right with You . . . and with Miss Cedar, but, to be straight up, I'm not doin' it for her. I'm doin' it for me.

"If she up and rides off and leaves me, You got to promise not to leave me, too. And I promise if she turns me down, I won't leave You neither. And You know that my word's good."

He took a big deep gulp of fresh air and then glanced back at the sun as it dropped behind the purple western mountains. He took it slow climbing back down the rocks to Brownie.

Swinging into the saddle, he began to whistle.

He was still humming a tune several hours later when he turned out the lantern and flopped on his back in the hard wooden bed. He reached to the bedpost and groped for his holster and the grip of his revolver. Finding it in place, he dropped his right arm over the edge of the bed and located the Winchester lying on the floor.

Then he turned over and went to sleep.

The next morning Andrews had built a fire, boiled coffee, taken care of the horses, scratched the cat's head, and was in the kitchen frying salt pork when a shout startled him.

"Hatcher! Ho . . . the house! Tap, I know you're home. I can smell the bacon."

He buckled on his bullet belt and holster. Swinging open the front door, he was surprised to find a buckboard with two saddle horses tied to it parked in the front yard.

"Stack? What in the world are you doin' here?"

"Now that's a fine greeting. Here I am bringing home your two ponies, and I suppose you aren't even goin' to invite me in for breakfast."

"Get in here and grab your fork. 'Course, I'll have to cook another hog to fill up that frame of yours."

"Now you ain't goin' to charge me a dollar, are ya?" Stack needled.

"Nope. Two dollars. Grab some coffee while I'm cookin'. Then sit down here and explain yourself. You're supposed to be a day's ride away."

"Things happened fast after you left," Stack reported. "The Reverend and me took the whole bunch — livin', dead, and in between — into Fort Collins."

Tap waved a large fork in his hand. "Say, how's that gal — April?"

"Doin' fine. She went to Fort Collins with us, and a doc fixed her up. She just needs some rest. But here's the scoop. Them old boys had a reward on them — one hundred cash dollars a head." Reaching inside his vest, Stack pulled out a wad of greenbacks. "It's for you, Hatcher — five hundred dollars!"

"I won't take it," Tap said matter-of-factly.

"What do you mean, you won't take it?"

"I won't take a penny unless my partner takes half."

"What partner?"

"The one who helped me corral that bunch."

"Me?"

"Half of it's yours, or we send the whole amount back to the sheriff in Fort Collins."

"Well . . . I, eh . . ."

"Is it a deal?"

"If that's the way you want it." Stack divided the money into two piles and stuffed one back in his pocket.

"Now take another fifty and pack it back to the dance hall."

"What fer?"

Andrews pitched a plate of salt pork and fried bread onto the table.

"Give it to that dark-haired girl."

"Selena?"

"Yeah . . . that's the one. She's had some tough breaks, and she probably could use it."

Stack smiled and took fifty dollars off the pile. "You'll spoil her, givin' her better than she deserves, Tap."

"Yeah . . . well, we all need to be spoiled ever' once in a while, don't we?" Andrews sat down and speared a large bite of salt pork on his fork. "So what else is new?"

"Well, April closed down the dance hall for two weeks and gave the girls some time off. When I was in Fort Collins, I saw a handbill about an auction at a dance hall up near Halt."

"Halt? Where's that?"

"As near as I can figure, about a day's ride to the northeast."

"Over the summit?"

"That's what I figure. There was a mining concern out of Wyomin' that operated in there for a couple years. Then it went bust. I guess the dance hall went on for a while, but finally folded. April wanted me to buy what I could."

"But how did you get here so early in the mornin'?"

"A couple of Beckett's boys — say, did I tell you the reward for him is five hundred cash dollars, dead or alive? Anyway, they told me that when the gang robbed a bank in Wyomin', they would ride down to Halt, get a relay, ride over to here to Tucker's ranch for the second relay, and then down to April's. They claimed there was an old minin' road through the forest that allowed them to get here in less than a day. And they were right. But I didn't leave until almost noon, so I camped in the woods last night and rolled in here this mornin'."

"You'll have to show me the way. It might come in handy if I need to get to Fort Collins or Denver. Now what are they sellin' up at that auction? I could use a few things around here since the housewarming they gave me."

"Oh, you know — tables, chairs, beds, dressers, wardrobes, roulette wheels, pots, pans, flatware, lamps, lanterns, faro layouts. I guess a little of everythin'. 'Course, if I got that date wrong, it might all be gone when I get there."

"Do you suppose they'd have any mattresses and bed springs worth using?"

"Miss April said it was a fine place, and they had top-quality furnishin's. That's why she's sending me up there. Why, they even have one of them big grand pianos! 'Course, that would take up too much of the dance floor. If you don't get more furniture, you could put a grand piano in that front room of yours," Stack teased.

"Piano! She plays a piano! I almost forgot. I'm going with you, Stack."

"Well, that's mighty fine, Tap. But . . . eh, I'll have to go on up to Laramie for a few things before a swing down Virginia Dale way and into Fort Collins to pick up April."

"No, no, I'll take my own rig. I've got Bob McCurley's buckboard, and I'll go up there and buy a few things." Andrews picked up the remains of the reward money and folded it neatly into his vest pocket.

"It will be good to have some company on the trail. But I figure there will be a few trees and rocks to move, so maybe we better head out soon," suggested Stack.

"You're right. Imagine that. Won't Pepper be surprised when I bring home a piano?"

"Is Miss Pepper here?" Stack asked. "I ought to pay my regards."

"Here? Of course not. She's at McCurley's hotel until the weddin' . . . whenever that may be."

"Oh . . . yeah . . . well, thanks for breakfast. I'll go water my team." Stack started toward the front door and then stepped back into the kitchen. "Tap, there's somethin' I can't figure. Why do you want a big old piano for Miss Pepper? She don't know how to play. I'm the only piano-player in that dive, you know."

Andrews jerked his head around. "What are you talkin' about? Of course, Miss Cedar knows how to play. She said so in her letters . . . What's you and the dance hall got to do with that?"

"You mean she ain't never . . ."

"What are you talkin' about?"

"Well . . . eh, sorry about that, Hatcher, I guess I just got confused. I, eh . . . I thought you two were a talkin' and everything was straightened out now."

"Straightened out? Oh, yeah, that's true. We got everthing on the level now . . . as you probably figured out."

"Listen," Stack continued, while we're

gettin' your team hitched, why don't you tell me what it is you got straightened out? Sometimes I'm kind of slow. Maybe I missed a point or two."

Andrews tore off a piece of brown paper sack and scribbled a note with an extremely short stubby pencil. "Just in case Bob McCurley comes up here lookin' for his buckboard. I ought to let him know when I'm comin' back," he explained and then placed the note in the middle of the butcher block.

By the time both rigs rolled out toward the summit of the Medicine Bows, Tap had explained to Stack about his real identity. All the way through the conversation, Stack Lowery kept shaking his head and muttering, "I don't believe this . . . I just don't believe it."

They discovered an abandoned trail over the Medicine Bows that was rough going up, but still fairly smooth on the eastern slope. The country on the other side of the pass was treeless, windy, and barren as they approached what was left of the town of Halt.

It was late in the day, and freight wagons and buckboards lined the only street. Many were loading up everything from mining gear to windows and doors.

"At the rate they're tearin' this place

251

down," Tap said nodding, "there'll be nothin' left but a pile of splinters by mornin'."

"We was lucky to get here before they sold off the Green Slipper." Stack motioned toward the dance hall.

After several minutes of inspecting the merchandise, Tap met Stack at what was left of the bar — where a free supper was being dished out.

"Mr. Tap Andrews," Stack repeated. "Now I've got to get used to thinkin' of you as an Andrews. This is gettin' confusin'. You ain't goin' to tell me next you have a different name yet, are you?"

"Actually, Stack, my name is really . . . Stuart Brannon," Andrews joshed.

"I thought Brannon got shot down there in Tombstone."

"Nah, the Earps are in Tombstone. Brannons up near Prescott," Tap jibed. "Listen, Andrews is my birth name, and I don't plan on any more stretchers. Did you find Miss April some good possibles?"

"Mainly mirrors and chairs. A dance hall always gets mirrors and chairs busted up. How 'bout yourself? What are you goin' to carry back to the ranch?"

"Well, there's a couple of mattresses and springs sets that look good. If I can buy 'em both, I will. We can store one in the attic until we build on. Then I'll bid on a couple of those apple crates full of dishes. The boys pretty well busted up mine. And just for fun, I'll see if I can snag that piano."

"You're serious about it?"

"Yep. Listen, Stack. Answer me one thing. Can a man take those legs off?"

"Oh yeah, the legs is bolted on, and the bars down to the pedal unscrew . . . but I think . . ."

"What I was figurin' was this," Tap continued. "I'll sandwich it in good between those mattresses and then tarp it and tie it. But I'm not sure how to unload it when I get home. Guess I'll figure somethin' out when I get there. How much you figure it's worth?"

"I don't think you really want . . . well, worth? Oh, I suppose you'll have to spend a hundred dollars to get it."

"That's what I was figurin'. Normally I don't have that kind of silver, but with the reward money . . . well, it's been a good week!"

"You know, Andrews," Stack tried to caution, "what if Miss Pepper don't really . . . well, what if she don't like it? Or wanted a different style? Or maybe she just wants to up and retire from playing the piano. Then you'd be stuck with something mighty expensive fillin' up your front room."

"Stack, I know this seems a bit reckless, but I can just see Pepper sittin' at that piano in the evenin' playin' and singin' hymns —"

"Hymns . . . church songs?" Lowery choked. "Miss Pepper singin'? Oh . . . well . . . who am I to say? I guess you know what you're doin'."

"Stack, does it seem to you that we keep talkin' about a different lady?"

"Well, you are talkin' about the blonde in the buggy with the Reverend the other day, ain't ya?" Lowery quizzed.

"Certainly. Miss Suzanne Cedar. Now who are you talkin' about?"

Stack rubbed his two-day beard and pushed back his black hat. "Oh . . . look, I think they're about to start the auction. We best canter over there and get a good position. Maybe we can discuss this on down the road."

Tap's stomach knotted with anxiety.

He figured it was the lumpy mashed potatoes.

10

For two days Pepper paced her room, stared out the window to the north, and waited for Tap Andrews to return.

For two days she kept her hair carefully tucked in her combs, her boots laced up straight, and her dress unwrinkled — expecting to hear his voice at any moment.

For two days she memorized every tree, rock, sagebrush, and rabbit that scattered about the northern horizon.

For two days she took her meals in her room by the window. She didn't say ten words to anyone, nor did she venture more than fifty feet away from the hotel.

On the third day she stopped waiting.

Instead, she asked Bob McCurley to hitch the horse to the buggy, and she set out for the ranch without invitation or warning. Alone, the trip seemed unbearably long. Every mile was a repetition of brown grass, dust, and sage. The wide road grew narrow, and then it was just wagon ruts — some of which were slick with water held all year long. She closed her eyes for a few minutes, and when she opened them . . .

the scenery never changed.

All she had to do was try to stay awake in the mild, sunny day and do lots of thinking.

About her and Tap.

Over.

And over.

And over.

Lord, this is me. You know . . . Pepper? Well, I just can't take another day of this! I've got to tell him . . . I've got to tell him everythin'. It's beatin' me down. It's like a dark, heavy, horrible weight on my mind day and night. I'm not sleepin' much, and my stomach aches all day long. I've got to clear this up. Livin' this lie pains me now. I just feel like screamin'! Whatever happens will be better than this. Please, Lord . . . I'm going crazy thinkin' about it all the time. It won't let me go! Help me!

It was midafternoon when she turned north at the mouth of the canyon. When she crested the final ridge to the ranch, she was disappointed not to see any smoke from the chimney. As she approached the buildings, she searched for movement, but could see no more than Brownie and a couple of other horses in the corral and some multicolored cattle back up the draw. Stopping the carriage by the hitching post, she slipped to the ground and looped the reins to the brass ring.

Her legs felt stiff and sore as she tried to brush a little of the road dust off her newly acquired yellow dress.

"Tap, I will not come into the house nor unpack the carriage until I tell you," she muttered to herself as she approached the front door.

She banged on the door and glanced over to the barn. Finally, she pushed the door open a few inches.

"Tap? Tap? It's Pepper! Are you in here?"

He's probably out on the ranch somewhere. Now I'll have to wait to tell him. If I have to wait much longer, I'll scream!

The gray and white cat jumped off the front porch roof.

"Cat! You . . . you . . . oh, what's your name anyway? You scared me to death!"

The cat scooted past her and through the open door into the house. Following the cat, she entered the house, leaving the front door wide open.

"Well, cat, this room seems even bigger than I remembered . . . and empty." She peeked into the bedroom and then went to the kitchen.

Searching through the cupboards, she sighed, "Oh, Tap, they did bust up a lot of the dishes, didn't they?" She had turned to walk back to the front room when she noticed a scrap of paper on the butcher block in the center of the room.

Gone to Halt. Be back Thursday
night late.

Tap

*Gone to Halt? Where's Halt? Isn't that in
Wyomin'? Didn't one of the girls work there
once? Lord, I thought he wasn't goin' to see
the girls anymore. Why would he . . .*

"Today's Thursday!" she blurted out as
the cat jumped up on the butcher block
and rubbed its back on her arm. "He'll be
home tonight, cat, and we'll . . . we'll have
supper waitin' for him. I can cook, you
know. Well, maybe not as good as Danni
Mae, but a whole lot better than Paula or
Selena."

Pepper went out to get her valise. She also
brought in the two blankets and the shotgun that Bob McCurley insisted she carry.
Then she led the horse to the barn, parked
the buggy, pulled the tack off, and turned
the driving horse into the corral with
Brownie.

She built a fire in the fireplace to take
the chill out of the room. Then she shuffled
around the kitchen searching for food to
prepare.

She fashioned an apron out of a clean
flour sack. Soon coffee was boiling, and
sourdough biscuits warmed on top of the
cookstove. A thick stew bubbled, and a

cobbler made from dried apples filled the kitchen with a sweet aroma.

She stepped out the back door to dump some dirty water when she thought she heard a horse whinny in the front yard. Scurrying back into the house, she tossed down the pan, brushed her hair back with her fingers, and hurried toward the door. "Tap! Tap, you wait there. I need to talk to you right now! You don't get to take another step until —" The words were just slipping out of her mouth as she pulled open the door.

Suddenly a man's strong hand grabbed her arm, violently dragging her outside. The barrel of a revolver jammed against the flesh behind her right ear.

"Beckett!" she screamed.

"Now ain't this a surprise! Where is he? Where's that gunman that ambushed me? He's not in there, is he? 'Cause you was lookin' for him, weren't ya?"

"Turn loose," she shouted, "you're hurting me!"

"Oh, no, you blonde Jezebel, that ain't hurtin' ya." Then Beckett brought the back of his left hand slamming into her cheek and glancing into her shoulder. Pepper staggered back and fell to the porch. She grabbed her jaw and felt a trickle of blood on her cheek.

She didn't even consider crying.

"Now that's hurtin' ya!" He grabbed her

259

arm and yanked her back into the house, dragging her near the fireplace, finally releasing her on the floor.

"Beckett, you . . . you . . ."

"When's the gunman coming back?"

"If he finds you here, he'll kill you!" she warned. "You're dead. You know that, don't you?"

"Shut up!" he screamed.

She could smell the liquor on his breath.

"Somebody's going to die, all right, but not me. He's going to pay. He bushwhacked us, and he's goin' to pay!"

"Beckett, get out of here right now. I want you out of our house!"

"Our house? Our house? So you moved in with some back-shootin' gunslinger-loverboy?"

"I haven't moved in yet — not until we get married."

"Married? You . . . the yellow-haired dance-hall darlin'? Who in his right mind would marry you? You think he wants you for a wife? He's probably hopin' that you'll be gone before he comes back."

"That's not true!"

"It don't matter, 'cause when he walks through that door, he's dead."

"Don't count on it, Beckett."

"Oh . . . yeah, I'm countin' on you watchin' him die. After that, you and me, darlin', are ridin' off to Wyomin' where I'll teach you how you're supposed to treat a man."

"He whipped five of you. There's no way you'll get the drop on him."

"There were two of them, and they ambushed us. Not this time. He won't know I'm here, and I'll have a gun at your pretty little brainless head."

"That won't stop him. He'll kill you!"

"It'll stop him. I know the type. He's a jerk. Now, me . . . I don't really care whether I blow a hole in the side of your head or not. But that gunslinger . . . do you know why he didn't shoot me in the trees? 'Cause he was huggin' on that lyin', cheatin', knife-swinging breed of a dance-hall girl. He's too easily distracted. Why, I bet he don't give two bits which dance-hall girl he grabs."

Pepper jumped to her feet, yanked the iron fire poker, and took a wild swing at Jordan Beckett.

The outlaw slammed her hand against the wall. Pepper dropped the poker as a sharp pain shot right up to her shoulder. Then he twisted her arm behind her. It hurt so bad she was afraid it was breaking. She bit her lip until she could taste blood in her mouth.

She didn't scream.

She didn't cuss.

She didn't cry.

With one hand still forcing her arm up behind her and the other hand yanking her hair, he towed her across the room and shoved her into one of the straight-back wooden chairs next to the dining table. She felt him reach around and fumble at the back of her dress.

No! Please . . . Lord . . . no!

He tore off the flour-sack apron and used it to tie her hands behind her and then tied her to the chair.

Stepping back he leered. "Oh, don't you worry none, darlin'. I ain't going to damage the bait until after the fish is caught. Now when is this . . . this . . . I don't even know his name. When is he coming back?"

"His name happens to be Tap Andrews, and he's a professional shootist."

"Tap? What kind of name is that?"

"It stands for Tapadera."

"Tapadera? Is that Mexican? Have you got yourself a Mexican lover?"

"No, he's not Mexican. But what difference would that make? He's a professional gunman. He has a reputation down in Arizona."

"Good. It will be all the better that I'm the one who guns him down. And he ain't in Arizona anymore. Now when's this Tap comin' home?"

"It might be any minute . . . or it might be weeks."

"Honey, it don't matter to me. I've got plenty of time, but I don't think you're going to like sittin' in a chair for weeks."

"If I don't get back to the hotel tonight, they'll send men out to find me."

"Hotel? What hotel?"

"McCurley's."

"Let's face it, darlin', there ain't nobody who gives a nickel about a used-up dance-hall girl. Nobody is goin' to come lookin' for you. Nobody cares, and you know it. Whether I bury you in the ground or haul you off to Wyomin', nobody gives a —"

"God cares," she murmured.

"God? God! You got religion all of a sudden? That's a good one! There's only one place people like you and me are goin', and you know it."

He yanked the chair back, almost causing her to fall to the floor, and dragged her into the kitchen.

"Now, then . . . it looks like supper is cooked! Ain't that nice. And a big meal, too. Well, you figurin' on Mr. Fastshot eatin' soon? This is mighty nice. But since he won't get a chance to eat it, I might as well help myself. Hey, looky here . . . a pie." He grabbed a towel and pulled the pie out of the oven. Scooping out a plate of stew and bread, he began to smack and gobble it down.

"If you ride off right now, Beckett, I won't

even tell him you were here," she bargained.

He stared at her for a moment and then continued to eat. He marched out to the front room, peered out the front window, and then returned to the kitchen, banging open the cupboards.

"Where's the likker? Where does he keep the bottle?"

"He don't drink."

"You believe that lie? Every gunslinger on this earth takes a stiff belt."

"Not Andrews." She tugged at her bonds as she talked.

"And I suppose you're goin' to tell me he's got religion, too?"

"Perhaps he has."

"Good. Then you won't mind me puttin' a bullet in his brain and sendin' him to his heavenly reward."

He dragged the chair, with Pepper still tied in it, back to the front room. Using the towel to protect his hand, he brought the pie and a fork and tossed them on the table. Then Beckett took the towel, jammed it in Pepper's mouth, and tied it behind her head.

"Now I wouldn't want you hollerin' at your boyfriend, would I?"

He paced the floor of the house with his revolver in his right hand, constantly glancing out the windows in all directions.

Lord, I've got to tell Tap . . . before I die

. . . before he dies. I've got to tell Tap who I am. I've got to tell him I love him. I've got to tell him how much I want him to learn to love me, too. Lord, just that . . . just that much. Please God, I don't deserve it, but . . . but . . .

By the time the pie had cooled, it was dark. Beckett closed the thin front-room curtains. Then he lit a lantern and set it on the table in front of Pepper.

"Now we want a nice friendly shadow greetin' your beau, so maybe we ought to do some rearrangin'."

Beckett stepped close to Pepper. She tried to shout through the gag. He pulled the combs out of her hair, and she could feel his dirty fingers running through it.

"Well, darlin', how nice . . . that's a lot more friendly. Now just one more adjustment." He yanked her hair back, forcing her chin toward the ceiling. She struggled to see what he was doing. Beckett pointed his Colt at her neck. Then he shoved the hard, cold steel barrel of the revolver between her skin and the high collar of her dress. He turned the barrel so that the gun sight caught the material of her clothing. Then he jerked the pistol back, ripping the top several buttons off the yellow cotton dress.

"Now . . . isn't that more comfortable. Why you look like the kind of dance-hall

265

girl any dumb, drunken cowboy would be interested in."

I don't want to be here, Lord. Take me away . . . please! Don't let Tap find me like this!

For almost an hour Beckett sat there with his revolver cocked, pointed at the front door, and lying on the table. He forked the pie and described in detail how much fun he and Pepper would have once the shooting was over.

Both of them jumped when they heard the squeak of a buckboard roll into the yard. Pepper's heart pounded so loud that it ached. She thought she would pass out.

She didn't.

Beckett stayed away from the window, making sure Pepper was between him and the door. His revolver was now pointed at her head.

She could hear the jingle of spurs as someone ran across the yard. She wanted to shout, to run to him, to wake up from a bad dream.

"Pepper! Pepper, you're here! Come out here and see what I bought you." He shoved open the front door and stepped inside. "You'll be able to sing and —"

"You go for your gun, mister, and your dance-hall girlfriend is dead. Do you hear me?"

"Beckett?" Tap gasped. "What's goin' on?

266

Pepper?" Tap didn't try for his gun, but his eyes searched the room for other hidden men.

"Are you all right?" he asked her.

She nodded.

"Beckett, you're a dead man. You can put all six shots in me, but I'll still have time to put one between your eyes!"

"That's what your hurdy-gurdy gal keeps tellin' me, but I just don't believe it."

Pepper's heart sank. Every word Beckett spoke crushed her spirit.

No, Lord . . . don't let him find out this way. Please. I've got to tell him. Lord, You promised me a chance. Lord, please, not this way!

"Go ahead, gunslinger, pull your .44! Let's just see how good you are. I say I can put a bullet through her head before you clear your holster. Go ahead. Do it!"

Tap's eyes searched the room for anything that would give him some advantage.

"Here's the last laugh, Mr. Tap Andrews. When you're laying there on the floor dead, Miss Pepper Paige will be ridin' off with me. But that's what's so fun about dance-hall girls, ain't it? They don't care who they're with . . . as long as he has money. Why, me and Pepper, we go back a long time, don't we, darlin'? We used to spend many a wild time at April's. She was all the boys' favorite, yes sir. But her heart belonged to me. But then she soured and packed up and left."

Pepper couldn't hold it back any longer. Even with a gag in her mouth, she began to sob.

Lord, have him shoot me . . . Shoot me, Beckett! I don't want to live! Not now. Not like this. Oh, please, Lord, let me die!

She wanted to reach around and wipe her eyes, but her hands were tied, and she could tell there were no tears.

"Come on, gunslinger!" Beckett screamed. "Make your move! I'll show you who's the best! The winner gets the dance-hall darlin' — at least until she rides off with some California gambler."

"It's your play, Beckett. What's the matter?" Tap heckled. "You don't have the nerve, do you? You didn't think this through too good, did you? You know that if you shoot the girl, I'll have a bullet through you before you ever have that hammer pulled back again. So you've got to shoot me first, don't you? But if you only hit me in the body, I'll have plenty of time to lead you down. That means you've got to aim for my head. Of course, if you miss . . . you're dead, and I don't have a scratch. Are you that good a shot? Huh, Beckett, are you that good? Maybe sober, but how about half-drunk? Can you do it, Beckett? Or do you just limit yourself to beatin' up dance-hall girls?"

Andrews stared at Beckett's eyes in the flickering lantern light. Suddenly the gray and white cat, who had been sleeping in the kitchen, romped across the room toward Tap.

Jordan Beckett nervously jerked his gun, squeezing the trigger and slamming a bullet into the floor.

Tap Andrews never took his eyes off Beckett.

The .44-40 missed Pepper by no more than four inches and caught Jordan Beckett about a quarter of an inch above the right eyebrow, driving him against the back wall.

Pepper let go with a muffled scream.

Tap jumped to get between her and Beckett, cocking the revolver as he did. His precaution was not needed. Beckett's lifeless body slumped to the floor.

Jamming the gun back into his holster, he spun around to untie Pepper's hands and then her gag.

Her tearless sobbing was uncontrollable. She tried to catch her breath. She tried to keep her hands and arms from shaking.

Tap grabbed her, picked her up in his arms, and, kicking the door open, carried her outside.

He's going to put me in the carriage and make me go back. Lord, I didn't even get a chance to explain.

She tried to speak, but nothing came out.

Tap carried her to the bench on the front porch and sat her there. Then he sat down beside her and held her close to him. With one arm slipped around her waist and the other entwined in her tousled blonde hair, he pressed her head to his chest.

Neither said anything for a very long time.

When she finally looked up, the moon was just bright enough that she could see that he was staring out into the night.

Her voice was weak and trembling. "Why did you leave McCurley's without seein' me? You knew I wanted to talk to you. Why didn't you come back? I prayed and I prayed that I would have a chance to tell you. Oh, Tap . . . he was right. Beckett was right. I'm just a dance-hall girl. I was tryin' to fool you, too. I'm not Miss Suzanne Cedar. I can't be her, Tap. Oh, God, I wish I could be her. I wish you could have loved me the way you loved the lady in those letters. I tried . . . but I don't know how. I never learned how to do it right. Oh, Jesus, help me now . . . Help me, please. I hurt so bad I just want to die! Oh, God, I want to die!"

He didn't loosen his grip, but spoke in low, soft tones.

"Aimee Paige, you hush up for a minute and let me tell you a story."

"You . . . you know my real name?"

"Let me tell you what I know. Aimee was born in Georgia. Her daddy died defending Atlanta. Her mama remarried a man named Bonner Hopkins. He had four boys all older than her. They moved to Nebraska, then to Nevada, then to Florence, Idaho."

"Who told you —"

"Just wait," Tap continued. "Aimee's mama got real sick in Florence, and Aimee had to cook, clean, sew, and wash for Hopkins and his sons. When she was fourteen, her mama died, and Hopkins, who worked long hours in the mine, used to come home drunk every day." Still holding her close, he looked down at her blonde hair. "How am I doin' so far?"

Keeping her head against his chest, she nodded for him to continue but said nothing.

"Well, after one week of several beatings from Hopkins, she was cornered in a barn by two of her stepbrothers who tried to tear off her dress. She stabbed one in the leg with a pitchfork, and the other she whacked along the side of the head with an axe handle.

"She left town that day with a man who took her as far as Boise City, where he promptly got caught cheatin' in a card game and was shot and killed while she looked on.

"After some weeks of stealin' food scraps and sleepin' out under a bridge, she took a job in a dance hall. By then she was still only fifteen. Since then it's been dance halls in Idaho, Montana, Wyomin', Nevada, and Colorado.

"Then one day while she worked for April Hastings in Pingree Hill, a severely injured lady named Suzanne Cedar was brought into the dance hall. This lady had come west to marry a rancher named Zachariah Hatcher. When the lady died in her room, Aimee decided to pretend to be Miss Cedar.

"She does a good job of foolin' the rancher, but then finds out that the man is not Hatcher, but just a driftin' shootist by the name of Tap Andrews, who happens to be an escaped prisoner."

He paused for a moment.

"How's my story?" he asked.

"Painfully accurate," she admitted. "Who told you all that? How long have you known?"

"Oh, I've known those details for about twenty-four hours, but I didn't really believe it . . . until just now. Stack Lowery went with me to the auction, and he told me the story."

"Stack! How could he?"

"Don't blame Stack. He was under threat. It just slipped out at first. He didn't want me to buy the piano — told me that Pepper couldn't play or sing."

"I can't. But there's some of the story you don't know."

He sat her up and released his grip. "All right, tell me the missing parts."

"Keep holding me," she requested softly.

"What?"

"Treat me like I was a hurting dance-hall girl having a bad week. Hold me gentle."

Tap pulled her back into his arms.

"All that you heard is close enough to the truth. I'm not goin' to tell you more about it because I don't ever want to think about those days again. But Stack couldn't tell you about the night that Suzanne Cedar died in my arms. She was ever'thing I wanted to be but never had the chance. She loved Hatcher dearly and yet trusted her Jesus right up to the end. She told me she thought I was an angel sent from God to take care of her.

"When she died, I got to readin' those letters from Hatcher . . . and something inside of me made me want to get out of the dance hall and be like her. Well, the next night Beckett came in drunk as usual. He started treatin' me mean, and I put him down. I quit at the same moment that April fired me. Having nothin', and with no place to go, I contrived the scheme to pretend I was Miss Cedar and see how far I could take it.

"Only I didn't count on Mr. Hatcher being so handsome and exciting and caring. In a matter of days, I loved not only the dream but the man also. Meanwhile I was reading Miss Cedar's Bible, trying to be like her. All of that readin' got me convinced that maybe the Lord was leading me in all this."

She stopped as her voice started to falter.

Tap rocked her back and forth in his arms. "You don't have to say any more if you don't want to."

"He forgave me, Tap. Do you know what that's like? God really did forgive me for all of that! That's when I made my pledge. I was so anxious to find you and tell you the truth.

"But then we heard the shots and found you in that gunfight. You dragged me over to them trees and wouldn't let me say anythin'. I was so shocked to hear your story I didn't know what to do next. I know you are crazy in love with that Cedar woman, and I just couldn't stand to have you put me out. I've been put out lots of times, Tap. I didn't think I could take it again.

"But for two days I haven't slept and couldn't eat. I had to talk to you, but you didn't come back to McCurley's . . . so I came out here. And I fixed your supper. Then Beckett showed up.

"I was really scared — more scared than

ever before. Most of the time in the past ten years I haven't cared whether I lived or died. But tonight I was afraid you would be killed. It scared me real bad . . . real bad.

"But I'm not her, Tap. I'm not the girl you're in love with. I'm not that good, that refined, that proper, that pure. I'm goin' to do my best, but I'll never be Suzanne Cedar. I'm just Pepper. But I'm forgiven. Honest, I am!"

Tap continued to rock her back and forth.

Neither spoke a word.

The gray and white cat, which had disappeared into the darkness at the explosion of gunfire, now wandered back to the house and jumped up into Pepper's lap.

She petted it.

The cat purred.

Andrews remained silent.

"Tap . . . please, talk to me. Say somethin'. You can tell me the truth. I can take it now. I'm not just another Selena who needs a hug and a kiss before you leave. I'm goin' to make it. Things are different. I'm different."

By now the air was growing cold, and the stars were bright. An almost-full moon had risen in the eastern sky, and the western mountains reflected its glow.

Standing up, Andrews pulled Pepper to her feet. The cat scampered down the porch. "Come here," he said and walked to the western end of the south-facing porch.

"You see that range of hills over there?"

"Yes."

"That's the edge of the ranch. Well, right on the southern end is a butte made up mostly of exposed granite. A couple of days ago I hiked up to the top of that. From there you can see into Wyomin' in the north and clear to McCurley's hotel."

"What were you doin' up there?"

"Thinkin' about you . . . me . . . and God."

"God?"

"Been readin' some of Hatcher's Bible, you know, in order to impress Miss Suzanne Cedar. Well, it got me to thinkin' real hard. And . . . I decided it's about time for me to take Jesus serious whether you agreed to marry me or not. Pepper, this is hard for me to talk about."

"But that was before you visited with Stack . . . what about now? Tap, what's goin' to happen now?"

Still holding her hand and looking at the western hills, he paused for a long time.

"We're quite a pair . . . aren't we? We got nothin'. We've done nothin' we want anyone to remember. We got a past that we'll spend a lifetime tryin' to outlive. We're tied to no one and no place — with absolutely nothin' awaitin' us in the future. What a team of losers."

"I don't feel like a loser right now," she offered.

Andrews gazed into her eyes. "I'm goin' to get it right this time. Pepper . . . will you consider marryin' this reckless gunfighter who's tryin' to change his ways?"

"Who are you askin' — Miss Suzanne Cedar or —"

"I'm asking Aimee Paige, who used to be a wild dance-hall girl. And if she doesn't hurry up and say yes, my stomach's goin' to split in two with worry!"

"Do you mean that?" she asked.

"Yep."

"You ain't just feelin' sorry for a dance-hall girl, are you?"

"Nope."

She slipped her arms around his neck and pulled herself up on her toes so she could place her lips on his. When she pulled back, she started to cry. It was a deep, rolling, uncontrollable sob. She struggled to catch her breath.

Then she reached up to brush her eyes. The tears flooded over her fingers and across her face.

"Look," Tap insisted, "I don't know if you're cryin' 'cause you're happy or cryin' 'cause you're sad. Are you going to say yes or no? Which is it?"

She continued to wail.

"Tell me, are you goin' to marry me?" he demanded.

"Yes, yes!" She let out a deep cry, shaking her head up and down.

"Yes? You will? You said yes?"

She continued shaking her head up and down while tears rolled off her cheeks, dripping on her torn dress.

Suddenly she threw her arms around his neck and hugged him so tight that he thought he would lose his breath. In a moment she released her grip and stopped crying.

They stood there staring into each other's eyes for a considerable time. Finally, it was the cat meowing and rubbing against their legs that caused them to stand back.

She looked out into the yard and then turned to him. "What was it you bought me?"

"A big grand piano."

"A piano? But . . . I don't know how . . . that was Suzanne. After you had that discussion with Stack, how come you went ahead and bought it?"

" 'Cause I . . . I, eh . . . didn't like the looks of the other old boy who was biddin' on it."

"What?"

"And I figured you could learn how to use it."

"Me — play the piano?"

"Oh, it can't be all that hard. I can tell you're the type that can do anything you set your mind to."

"I am?"

"Sure. You snagged me, didn't you?" he teased.

"Me? You're the one who come around beggin' me to marry you!" she protested.

"So that's the story you're goin' to tell all our friends?"

"Tap Andrews, we don't have any friends."

"Well," he said smiling, "we both, eh . . . are mighty friendly with dance-hall girls."

Her tight-fisted right cross caught him in the stomach. Laughing and gasping, he pushed her back. "Okay . . . okay. No more joking about the girls."

Pepper reached down and scooped up the gray and white cat.

"You two stay out here," he ordered. "I've got to clean up the house a little and escort our house guest outside."

"Before you do that, I've got one question."

"I hope it's an easy one."

"What's the name of this cat?" Pepper asked.

"Name? Eh, I was hopin' you'd know its name."

"Me?"

"I mean, I was hopin' Miss Suzanne Cedar knew its name. He was here when I first came to the ranch."

"Well, we'll have to name him," she insisted.

"Then let's call him Salvation." Tap shrugged. "I reckon he saved us from Beckett's bullet."

Pepper squinted her eyes and wrinkled her nose. "But I read somewhere in Suzanne's Bible that 'salvation belongs to the Lord.' "

"That's fine with me." Tap shrugged. "He's sure not my cat!"